DANCING WITH A STRANGER

Pauline Plummer

Short Stories

RED SQUIRREL PRESS

First published in the UK in 2015 by Red Squirrel Press
www.redsquirrelpress.com

Red Squirrel Press is distributed by Central Books Ltd.
and represented by Inpress Ltd.
www.inpressbooks.co.uk

Cover designed by Alan Turnbull
turnbull.fineart@btinternet.com

Copyright © Pauline Plummer 2015

The right of Pauline Plummer to be identified as the author of this work has been asserted by her in accordance with Section 77 of the Copyright, Designs and Patents Act 1988. All rights reserved.

A CIP record is available from The British Library.

ISBN: 978 1 906700 980

Printed by Martins the Printers
www.martins-the-printers.co.uk

Contents

Meeting Madonna	7
Syrah	19
Visiting Room	27
Light Work	39
Snow on Snow	57
The Sea-coloured Gown	67
The Queen of Sheba	75
The Stone Dress	87
Back	93
Landscape	103
Sword Beach	113
Jerome	123
The Frock	127
Goebbels' House	139
What You Need For Happiness	147
Oasis	159
Odelia	167
Kaya	177

Also by Pauline Plummer
from Red Squirrel Press

Poetry:
Bint
(2011)

'A man who works with his hands is a labourer. A man who works with his hands and his head is a craftsman. A man who works with his hands, his head, and his heart is an artist.'

'What we are looking for is what is looking.'

'We have been called to heal wounds, to unite what has fallen apart, and to bring home those who have lost their way.'

- St Francis of Assissi

Meeting Madonna

Sister Mary passed a plate of birthday cake to Neneh, a very dark woman with an oval, serious face and asked her to share out slices to each priest in the convent sitting room.

Rosie was too hot to eat, her face red and sweating.

'The climate takes a bit of getting used to,' whispered the nun to Rosie. 'Go on and take a shower. No need to be here.'

'I didn't know bishops could be so jolly.'

'Sure you don't know what he survived when he was captured by the rebels.'

The sun came in at sharp angles through the high windows. It was late afternoon in May and the air smelt of ripe mangoes. There was a power cut so the caretaker turned on the generator. Its gravelly hum drowned the noise of the cicadas.

After she'd cup-showered and changed into shorts and crop top, Rosie leaned over the balcony watching and she was still there as Sister Mary climbed up the concrete stairs.

'Look at you. You'll get bitten and, well, respectable girls here don't show their bellies.'

Rosie's face turned the colour of cheap red wine and she hurried up the passageway to her room torn with embarrassment and resentment. Why had she come at all?

Early morning was cooler with a breeze blowing in from the Atlantic, spreading the curtains wide like wings. The fan whirring in the kitchen reminded Rosie of wood pigeons coo-cooing in Victoria Park, near her home in London. She looked over a mug of tea at Neneh tying a rectangle of wax-patterned cloth around her chest, to protect her clothes from the cooking.

'You could help in the school today,' said Sister Mary. 'There are some big boys who can't read well so can't move on to secondary. We have some readers – based on life here.'

She nodded but she was beginning to wonder exactly what she could do – she couldn't give injections, she couldn't cook a hot pepper soup and she wasn't a trained teacher. This whole thing was a bad bad idea.

The school was just beyond the compound and as they crossed beyond the two huge mango trees they could hear the children's voices in chorus. The classroom had no glass in the windows but it was dark and shadowed inside, packed with children behind rows of old, scarred desks. The teacher held a long switch but even so they swivelled to stare and whisper at Rosie. The sisters were all old but the girl with shiny, red hair and large freckles was extraordinary. Three big boys from the back row carried chairs out to a mango tree. She sat with them as they concentrated on their reading books, the compound echoing with carefully pronounced, deeply resonating, vulture, chicken, barracuda, snake....

At the end of the session she crossed to the kitchen

where a queue of old, destitute women in patched gowns stood at the gate, which Sister Mary came out to open. Neneh spooned rice and stew into plastic bowls, which were passed around. There was one young woman, skinny, in a grubby dress, who touched the nun's arm. She flinched.

'Remember me Sister? Madonna. I need money to see my children in Guinea.' Her skin was taut over the bones of her face, her hair fashionably short and straightened. She was as thin as a faun. With her hand curved in a beckoning gesture, she turned to Rosie and whispered 'Nice skin. Pretty girl. Give me some money so I can go to see my children in Conakry.'

Rosie was unsure what to do. She sometimes gave to beggars in London, especially if they were playing music. Who was she?

'Why are your children there?'

'The war. You know we all had to run and got split up. I sent them with a relative to a refugee camp in Guinea. Me I had to stay and earn.'

It was hard to take in the enormity of war, when people talked about it in such a matter of fact way. It happened. They'd lived through it and Rosie just picked up bits and pieces of their stories, that they were shared over a meal or a walk.

'What do you do?' she asked, trying to turn the conversation into something normal.

'Well sometimes I help out in a bar. I dance too. And I speak not bad French.'

Rosie wondered why she looked grubby when even the hawkers, with bowls of mangoes on their heads, looked spotless.

'You could lend me. You come from a rich country. Where do you live?'

'London.'

'I have family in London too – maybe they will send for me. We could be friends there.' She gave a low throaty laugh and coughed.

'Do you have cigarettes?'

'No smoking allowed here. I could lend you some money. But you'll pay me back won't you?'

Madonna's symmetrical bones and almond eyes curved up and Rosie saw how beautiful she was. She pulled out some damp Leone notes from the pocket of her jeans. Madonna turned and was gone like a wraith.

Sister Mary, with her blue head scarf tied on, came out with a bag of medicines and syringes that she was taking to the clinic.

'Has that woman gone?'

'The one with the short dress?'

'A sad case. Too much of this.'

'This?'

'Can't you tell the girl's a prostitute? Poverty reduces girls to this sometimes. She's come here before begging, perhaps for drugs, perhaps just somewhere to sleep. God knows. Some of these girls lived in abandoned cars in the wreckers' yards but even for this they pay in kind. She's so thin, I wonder if it's Aids.'

They walked in silence along the main road. The pavements were full of people trading in cooked snacks, rolls of bright coloured cloth, plastic flowers, soap and second hand shoes. They avoided the open storm drains and turned into side streets, where the houses piled up haphazardly, like detritus washed in by a storm. Toddlers chased about. A woman with a baby on her back pounded cassava leaves in her mortar to a soundtrack of religious reggae, blasting from a radio. Rosie felt the rhythm of her stride change as she synced with the music and her spirits lifted. She smiled at her companion.

'I thought when I came to Africa I'd be like dancing and hearing music non stop.'

'Early days yet. You have time to go to wedding parties and so on. Go to Mass on Sunday, and you'll hear some wonderful singing and drumming.'

'Well, I wasn't thinking of church music, quite.'

The nun laughed.

'Or go with Neneh to her evangelical service. Plenty of music there. Too noisy for me, oh.'

'I was wondering about going clubbing or dancing – you know, some fun.'

The nun sighed. 'Your mother didn't tell me why you left the University. Here young people are desperate to get on in education.' She wiped her face with the blue headscarf as they climbed up a rough, red earth track to the clinic. A queue of adults and children were already waiting outside in the sun.

'How de body Sister?' they called out and she greeted back in Krio, turning to Rosie. 'You can cut up some bandages and get out some needles for me.'

The first patient was a toddler with a high fever. Sister looked her over as she lay listless in her mother's arms and asked Rosie to find the Chloroquine tablets. The next was a man with an infected gash in his arm. Rosie, swallowing her squeamishness, helped clean it up and bandage it.

When the muezzin called from the mosque the sky was a pattern of mauves and reds, dramatic and fiery. They made their way home through streams of children in green uniforms, back from afternoon school, the girls with berets balanced at precisely the right angle to the face.

'So, how's today been?' Sister drank water from the fridge and splashed her face.

'Interesting. Can I go out sometimes in the evening?'

'Not by yourself Rosie, it wouldn't be safe. Maybe you could make a friend or two and go to a café on the beach.

Students go to the British Council for events.' She rolled her eyes and turned to look at Neneh, who was sat filleting the small bones from a smoked fish. Rosie's spirits sank. Was she going to be locked up here for six months, how uncool was it going to be?

'Fine gal oh, be careful we u de go na town oh.' Neneh gave that low key, cautious smile of hers, her obsidian eyes flickering with light, or was it amusement, Rosie wondered.

She took her beer out into the cool of the compound and sat by a hibiscus bush, where she heard tapping behind her. Madonna was there again, at the wrought iron gate. She had changed into cleaner clothes and beckoned with long fingers through the bars.

'Girl. You like to come with me to see Freetown? The nuns don't know this city. The honey city.'

Rosie wanted to see something of the city. She hadn't come here to be canonised. Madonna reached for the beer but Rosie hesitated. Did she really want to drink from the same bottle? Too late, the long fingers pressed around it and removed it from her sweating hand.

She looked for her relative in the convent. 'Just going for a walk Auntie. I won't be long. I'll be fine. London's a tough city too you know.'

Sister Mary stood with her hands on her hips.

There were no streetlights, just the flames from the kerosene lamps that the street sellers lit by their stalls.

Madonna's skin glistened in the light. Rosie was glad of the dark. No one would be able to see how the seat of her jeans stuck to her buttocks.

They walked into the city centre, threading their way through the crowded pavements. Madonna stopped at a bar with sides made from bamboo mats.

'You have money? I like a beer.'

Rosie ordered them and she wiped the neck of the bottle as she saw the other woman do.

'You like hot pepper chicken?' She hissed for the waitress and a plate was brought. Rosie didn't think she had ever eaten anything so hot. They had more Star beers and Madonna pulled some cigarettes from her bra while they chatted about life in England.

Some older men came into the bar. They didn't look English with their olive skins and strong features, maybe Lebanese, and with them were two beautiful girls wearing tight two-piece dresses. One of the girls stroked the old man's inner thigh with her long fingers, as if pleading with him.

'This is how it is here. A girl has to find a man to ... to sponsor her, you know. Otherwise there is no way to buy clothes or pay rent or fees to study.'

'You don't have parents?'

'My mother left me here to go to England with her new husband, many years ago. My relatives passed me from one to the other. Always so many chores. Fetch this water, scour that pot, sweep that yard. I was so smart at school but sometimes they wouldn't pay the fees. I'm sure my mother sent money for that.' She spoke in a low, sibilant voice, devoid of emotion. Rosie was surprised how coolly she talked about what must have been so painful. To be left behind by your mother, with uncaring relatives, how did that affect you?

'So why have you left your children with people in Guinea?'

Madonna drew on her Marlborough and exhaled smiling but did not answer the question. 'You don't know what happened here in the war, do you? You will be my friend. I love you people. You can take a letter for me to England. I have a father in Kono. I think he may be still alive but he is ashamed of me.'

Rosie didn't want to think about fathers ashamed of their daughters. Her father was mad at her, it was true – she'd failed the second year of the degree, after all that hectic social life and intoxications and they couldn't afford her to repeat.

Madonna picked at her chicken and wiped her mouth and fingers on a tissue. 'Do you have a phone? I want to call my mother.'

'It doesn't work here.'

'You don't have Zain? Why not? You are rich, you can pay for this.'

'You're wrong. I'm just a failed student. My mother's a nurse. We're not rich.'

'You never go hungry? You eat butter every day? You have house?'

'Flat – with my parents and my brother.'

Madonna chewed on this information while Rosie studied the grooves down the sides of the mouth, the purple-brown bags under the eyes. She'd been aware in the first year of university, that when she looked at students' faces, she could see how they would be when they were older. But this girl was worn out already. She wanted what Rosie had had and lost.

Rosie looked around. The bar was filling up and the beer was making her cheerful. Well, at least she was out in town, with people and music, and a sense of anything is possible. The streets were heaving with crowds on the move.

A man stopped at the table and leant into Madonna's face whispering something but looked at Rosie while he did so. Then he sat down a few tables away but stared while he picked his teeth. Suddenly the noise seemed overwhelming and the beer had gone to her head. She felt dizzy. She didn't like the way the man scanned her up and down with a toothpick stuck between the gap in his front teeth.

'Lamin likes you,' said Madonna. 'We could all go to Paddy's Bar for the night. You can get us get a taxi. It's near Lumley Beach.' She beckoned to the man.

'But he's so old.'

He pulled a chair up beside her, his eyes glinting in the

light from the kerosene lamp. He shook Rosie's hand.

'What is your name?' She felt his thumb rubbing around on the inside of her palm and shuddered.

'Rose Murphy. I'm working with the nuns at St. Bernadette's Convent.' She said it crisply as if she were a novitiate herself. 'And I think I have to go back now. They will be expecting me.'

'So early, pretty lady? Let's all go and party. We Sierra Leoneans know how to enjoy ourselves.' He was still holding her hand and smiling, with the toothpick between his teeth. Rosie suddenly thought of the mess she'd got into in her hostel at the university and how it had all ended in her leaving. Please God not here as well. Do I want to go home she thought, maybe I'm getting out of my depth. But how to get home at night with no street lights?

A firm hand suddenly tapped her on the shoulder, a broad hand with a hard palm and she swivelled to see Neneh's dark face above the bamboo sides of the bar.

'Rosie I wan you fe go na house now. ' Her face was solemn. She had a deep voice and pronounced every syllable carefully, the way she cut cassava leaves into tiny portions. Madonna shrugged and looked away. Lamin sucked his teeth and held on to Rosie's hand. She thought of the story she could be telling back home if she stayed and went clubbing with these people. It might be fun, exciting in a reckless kind of way and she would see what people got up to behind the nuns' backs.

But she looked at Neneh's heavy, oval head and thought of the kindness in her and she couldn't be rude to such a woman. so she put out the cigarette and pulled her hand out of Lamin's grasp and followed Neneh's straight back into the street, still heaving with people, still waves of heat rolling up from the pavement, still flickering with kerosene flames and the smell of frying plantain. She felt foolish, like a girl in trouble with her parents, but also relieved to catch up with Neneh. She wondered if Neneh had followed her into town, worried about her safety. If so, then her kindness was special and Rosie felt embarrassed to have caused her this trouble. She was here. She would make the best of it. She matched her stride with Neneh's and they crossed through town and beyond, calmly chatting about ordinary things, until they reached where the convent lay still and peaceful under the stars.

Syrah

I'm lost in the rain walking back from the village across the undulating vineyard's fields to the barn where we sleep. The two vanilla slices in their paper bag are resting inside my rucksack along with bread, butter, jam and milk. The rain is warm as it falls on my burnt shoulders and arms. I stand under a poplar tree, the leaves trembling with raindrops, waiting for the shower to ease and a linnet is singing somewhere up in the branches.

Anita is hungry when I get back, especially because the Portuguese gang are grilling chicken in the yard, earthy smells of chicken fat, oregano and garlic. We sit on a bench inside the barn making sandwiches, drinking our free litre of wine that tastes of rusty metal. I hold the plastic cup up to my nose.

'I smell scrap yards, rag and bone men,' I say.

'A soupcon of dried blood,' says Anita. We are still giggling when Estevo comes over with two pieces of chicken but really it's for Anita. He can't just bring one. That kind of meanness isn't how the gang works. His English isn't great and Anita's Portuguese is non existent but he manages to persuade her with his Guinness coloured eyes to go for a walk, even though she, like me, is knackered from bending over vines all day in the heat, trying to keep up with the agricultural workers. My left hand has four cuts from the secateurs and one of them is looking nasty as if it's getting infected.

I take some soap and get a jug of water from the pump and give myself a flannel wash in the outhouse, chasing the peacock that's got in there. The vineyard owner loves peacocks so they're all over the farm, flashing their glittery feathers and stepping disdainfully. It feels good to swill off the sweat even though the water's cold. There's no point changing my jeans as there's nowhere to wash out purple stains from the grape juices so I just leave them on.

I shared a student flat with Anita in our second year in Liverpool, along with Mia and Sophie who have better things to do in late September (like enrolling) but Anita and I are not so well-heeled and we need more money to get through the semester. I know what Anita will be doing in the woods with Estevo. He's very beautiful but she hardly knows him. What is she like?

The Roma families are hanging out at the edge of the fields, the men playing cards and the women washing dishes in buckets. A guy who is nearly an old man beckons me over. He flicks a pack of tarot cards with one hand, so being bored I sit on the stool opposite.

'How much?' I say. I know they all speak a little English because we work side by side in the rows of vines. Estevo warned us, through miming, to hide our valuables because of the Ciganos. He showed us some loose boards at the back, where things could be hidden but I keep my money in a money belt under my jeans, just in case. I thought he was being racist but.

'20 euros,' says the old Roma.

I shake my head. 'I've only got 10.' I pull out a note from my jeans. That's two hours bent over in the vineyards so I'm definitely not paying more than that. He smiles a bit despite himself but I can't see his eyes as he's wearing black-dark, rimless sunglasses. He draws on his cigarette and passes me the cards to cut, then lays the first seven cards on the table. He picks up the first card and peers at it. His face is what I would call sepia, with thick black hair and a side parting but I can see a little grey at the roots so he must dye it. He points at the Queen of Cups. 'You save the world, I think,' he says. 'Like Mother Theresa.'

I humph under my breath. I just want to get through my course and get a half decent job. Sure I have dreams, I suppose, of working with Medecin Sans Frontiere but I'm not doing anything useful like medicine or nursing, just English and History.

He picks out another card and says 'You have raised a child.'

Well that would be my little brother. I was twelve when my mother died so really I had to take care of Simon, what with Dad being away a lot with his job and the drinking that went on, till he met Lizzie, my current stepmother. There's some more stuff about love and family, the children he sees me with, the man swinging his sword. Then he closes the pack. I guess time must be up. He points to the infected cut on my hand and shouts over in his language to one of the women. A few minutes later she puts a bowl of water on the table, takes out a clean piece of cotton and some kind of antiseptic and cleans it up, tut, tutting, muttering. A little girl, with the sweetest of faces comes to stand at the table watching. She has perfectly shaped, almond, amber coloured eyes in her light brown face. She has a green-patterned head scarf tied around and under the plait at the back. I ask her name in French and she understands and smiles.

'Lala,' she says.

By the time Anita gets back it's dark and I'm already in my sleeping bag on the hay, upstairs in the barn. She has bits of twig in her blonde-streaked hair. 'Goodnight,' I say and roll my eyes, pulling the sleeping bag over my head.

'Sorry, I didn't mean to leave you alone for so long but we walked down to the river. He's so sweet, such a gentle guy.' The moon can be seen through the window, casting shadows over the curving vineyards outside.

When the alarm goes off at five we have time for a quick face wash. Anita puts on the kettle and slices bread. We make a lunch to take to the fields and then we're ready out in the yard with the others, walking silently across the ridge of the first few fields we have already picked and into the next field. Dawn is rising over the hills, washing the earth in a soft pink light. The first rays of sunshine sparkle on dew-drenched Syrah grapes. The foreman arranges us across the field, so many people to a row and then we start moving, cutting bunches, dropping them into the sack. Though it was raining yesterday, the earth is dry and powdery. We have to concentrate to keep up with the Roma, who seem to fly down the lines of grapes. Some of the Portuguese gang are near us and throw grapes at us over the tops of the vines. Anything to bring some fun into this slavery. I see Anita and Estevo looking at each other through the vine leaves. If there was an orchestra in the copse of trees where the fields meet, they would be striking up violin music. Oh dear, she's in love again. Why does she give her heart away so easily? There was the sports centre coach last term and before that the creepy PhD student who was taking some of our seminars. At least Estevo is handsome and polite. Me, I keep my heart under lock and key. I'm not even sure if I know what the code word is. You can be sure that your brother, sister or cousin will be around for most of your life, in some way or even some of your girlfriends, the ones you've known since juniors but parents, you can't really rely on them to stick around, nor lovers or husbands.

These thoughts are flickering in and out of my head bent over, chop, chopping, snap, plop the smooth skinned grapes into the bag, feeling the weight of the juice inside, heavy with the richness they hold. I sing one or two favourite songs as we go along. 'Don't Worry' is an old fave and at least I remember the words to that one. I think my mum loved that song.

Lunch is under the shade of the trees in the copse. Estevo brings us over two cups of soup, which he has poured from a large thermos flask. The old Romany fortune teller is not in the line today but the woman who washed out my cut is there and I wave hello, smiling. I wish there was something I could give her to show my thanks and I fish out a Kit Kat from the bottom of the rucksack. Perhaps she'll like English chocolate, so I walk over and give it to her. She peels off the paper, snapping off one stick but the rest she puts in her pocket, probably for the kids. I can feel Estevo and the other Portuguese watching me while I do this. Why should I care what they think?

In the evening Anita and I are finishing off the cheap, new wine when Lala comes over from the Romany camp holding the rest of the Kit Kat. She smiles up at me. 'Merci,' she says softly and looks at us in a concentrated way, taking us in, as if she could swallow us with her eyes. I wave my hands and say 'Non plus,' which I think means, no more, in case she was hoping for more chocolate but she puts out her hand and touches my hand, looking at it, with its cuts. Then she runs her hand up my arm, and I realise she's looking at the freckles. I pat the top of her scarf-covered head and wish I had a toy, a ball or a balloon to give her. Perhaps when

I walk into the village on Saturday I'll look for something. Then I notice peacocks strutting into the barn and I chase them to see if I can get her a feather. Lala and I run round the barn and outhouse after them, laughing till I find one feather that must have fallen off. She waves it in the air as if was a sparkler and runs back to her camp.

In the village on Saturday, I wash my hair in the fountain in the square. I speak enough GCSE French to hear the muttered disapproval as the soap runs into the fountain and suds splash over onto the ground. Anita and I have a plate of frites and a beer in the café, anything would be better than the rusty red wine. Oh how good that is. I find a skipping rope in the village store. On Sunday I take it over to the Romany camp and ask for Lala. She is brought to me by the old fortune teller and her face lights up, when I pass the paper bag. I show her how to hold the handles and turn the rope, so she runs off looking for other children, probably to show off her prize. The old man turns to me.

'Lala has no mother,' he says. 'She is orphan.'

'Oh, really? How sad. Where is her mother?'

'Killed by a train.'

The next couple of weeks pass in a blur of aching backs and dirty clothes, cheap wine and Portuguese soup. I see Lala from time to time as she comes over to the barn to say hello, sometimes bringing me a perfect, light brown egg, still warm from the hen. I make her a paper swan from a magazine.

Anita and I go up to the big house to collect our wages and book a taxi to take us to the nearest town, where there is a train station. I've put on cleaner jeans and sweatshirt, let my hair hang loose, now I'm not working. Even a little makeup. Anita is sobbing in a corner after watching the van take the Portuguese gang away.

The woman who cleaned my cut comes to the barn door with a baby on her hip and Lala trailing behind. I think she's come to say good bye, so I put out my hand to shake hers but she takes my hand and puts it on Lala's shoulder. In broken French she tells me again, Lala has no mother, she has many children, I have none, I can take Lala to England, be her maman. I am aware of Lala's eyes fixed on mine, that unwavering stare, the glittering amber, the tilt of her face looking up.

'I'm a student,' I say. 'A student. I can't look after a child. I can't afford to keep myself.' But despite my mounting panic, I feel tears prick at the back of my eyes and I write down my name, address and phone number on a piece of paper, pressing it into her hand. 'Please write to me. Tell me how she is. I will speak on the phone and we will see.' I reach down and hug the little girl.

Visiting Room

'Mum, you're sitting on the wrong seat. You have to sit on the green. The remand prisoners sit on the blue.'

He reached for my hand and rested it on his remand jeans, looking at me, told me I'd put on weight and should take up jogging. I sat awkwardly on the hard, plastic stacking chairs breathing in the stuffy air, thick with cigarette smoke. The room was noisy, echoing with the screams of small children and loud, male voices.

'Do you get enough to eat? I brought some money if you want something from the snack bar.'

'Chocolate. As many bars and kinds of chocolate you can buy.'

I made my way through the clumps of families, aware that I looked and sounded middle class, out of it. At the counter I bought seven different kinds of chocolate bar and two cups of tea.

'Thanks mum. How's everything?'

'Much the same. I'm still doing ten hour days and year elevens are impossible but what can you do? They searched my hair when I came in here today and my mouth! What's it really like here Chris?'

'I'd prefer a cell on my own – the other guy's scary. Even the warders keep their distance. Mind you he had me shaving his head today. The cell stinks of cigarettes – and shit. You have to go in the corner behind a screen.'

I looked at his handsome face. Smiling. A row of perfect, even white teeth.

'Matt phoned. When he's home next weekend he'll come and visit. I've sent you in a Bible and arranged a daily paper to be delivered.'

'Not the Guardian? I'll be a laughing stock. The swotty black guy.'

'But with so many pages you'd have lots to read.'

'And why the Bible? Do you think I'm evil?'

He watched my expression, seriously and I looked back.

'No,' I said quietly. 'You got in with bad company. Has your Dad been to see you?'

'Yeah, I expect a lot of people'll come and visit me at first but if I get put away for a long time the novelty will wear off.'

Well, I thought, I won't be one of them, backwards and forwards to have my mouth and shoes checked in a queue, with the families of some of the kids I taught.

He wolfed down the chocolate as the time was ended. I wondered at the demons inside and thought of my own guilt. Who's ever a perfect parent?

'No lawyer been to see me Mum. I'm just a legal aid case. No bucks.'

The siren went and he marched back, turning to look as

he went through the door. I blinked back tears.

Outside the prison a heron flew overhead, the slow wing beat against a sharp blue winter sky. There was still frost on the grass and tiny shoots of snow drops beginning to crack through the heavy soil.

Before switching on the TV in the sitting room, I moved around the photographs of Chris on the mantelpiece – Chris as a baby with his teddy, Chris in a white ruffled shirt and shorts making his first holy communion, Chris in the school football team, Chris in sixth form with his hair in short dreads doing the rootsy thing. I opened a bottle and as the dark liquid slid down my throat, small tears slipped along the side of my nose, salt mixing with the metallic taste of cheap, red wine.

I woke up in the night sweating and panicked. A bad dream? I wondered about Chris in his cell. Was he safe? Was he suicidal? I writhed my worries into the sheets, until exhausted I fell asleep, Rags, his dog, snoring at my feet.

Although I was quieter than usual, my colleagues at the school hadn't noticed I was being eaten alive from inside. I caught myself listening more carefully to what the kids had to say, trying to understand what was behind their anger or rebelliousness or resentments.

'Didn't you think about what would happen if you got caught Chris?'

'Obviously not. Have you come to lecture me?'

'You've had so many opportunities. Books in the house, encouragement to admire black role models. Why were you hanging around with those dossers?'

'I can't cope if you're going to come and preach at me. And why can't you give Dad a lift here?'

He told me about the useful things he was learning, like how to heat up a can of baked beans by tearing off a strip of bed sheet, twisting it tight and lighting it so that it smouldered slowly under the can.

Even though he was officially an adult, I went to see his lawyer in the downtown offices, with their ripped plastic seating and dust covered desks. The lawyer's red, sports Jaguar was parked outside on the pavement. He had no idea who I was talking about when I mentioned the name.

'Mrs. Davis. There was a knife involved and one of the other defendants claims that Chris was holding it. It's not looking good.'

'But he insists that's not true. He went along for the ride. He's got no previous record.'

'But he's been hanging out with these guys. Perhaps he's been involved in other stuff and not got caught.'

I wondered whose side he was on. And I wondered if Chris was telling me the truth.

'Aren't you going to the prison to discuss the defence? Who are the jury going to believe? The mixed race youth from a single parent family or the local white working class boys?'

'Mrs. Davis this isn't a TV show. The next hearing will be about bail. I'll speak to him there.'

I walked home thinking about the thin line between those who got caught and those who broke the law but didn't get caught. How many times had I driven over the limit? I paid tradesmen in cash because they wouldn't pay tax on it and the bill would be cheaper. And Chris had grown up in what used to be called genteel poverty, shored up with credit card debt. I bottled up my other thoughts of what was too dangerous and sickening to know.

When I took the rubbish out, my breath made smoke in the night air. I spotted a falling star. Perhaps its light was a million years old. Perhaps it fell before pterodactyls turned into herons. What were they for these glittering stars, so remote and ancient shining on our messy lives, that fell out like a bag of old clothes at a jumble sale?

At school I saw a boy texting during the lesson and I threw a whiteboard marker in his direction. My head of department took me into her cupboard and made me a cup of tea.

'What's the matter Julie? You've great rings under your eyes.'

'The teacher, the thief, the beloved son, the useless father. Chris is in big trouble.'

She listened while I told her the story but she looked at her watch constantly and told me to go home and rest.

I drove home through a low fog that trapped all the factory

flares, smoke and car lights so that the fog was actually red, like driving through Hell.

I poured myself a glass of wine to do what Chris wanted me to do, so that when I phoned his father, my speech was slightly slurred.

'Winfield, we need to talk about visiting Chris.'

'We do, we do.'

'I wouldn't be calling you normally, as you know, but he wants to see more of you and I keep thinking about all the young men who commit suicide in prison.'

'Well, being black ain't going to help him…Babylon got him in its clutches.'

'This isn't about scoring points. God knows you haven't bothered much about him in the past.'

'You think I don't know?'

'Let's quit sparring and sort this out.'

I picked him up outside his house, turning away my head so I wouldn't have to see whatever woman was there. We drove to the prison in silence. I felt as though I would suffocate in the enclosed space of the car with the ex I hadn't seen for twelve years. There was the usual long wait for the visitors' numbers to be called, so it was impossible not to make small talk about his brothers and sisters and my brothers and sisters. Somehow neither of us could talk about what had or might have happened in the shop that was robbed. Chris beamed when he saw us both.

'Hey Pops, Hi Mum. Cool shirt Pops.'

Winfield smoothed the silk of his hand-painted shirt, in which the orange blazed into clouds of mauve and purple, like sunset over a lagoon.

'Y"have to dress to the occasion boy. No, seriously, Chris, you got yourself in a real mess. We doing what we can to support you. I know your mother doing her best.'

Years of sarcastic comments rose like bile but I forced them down. Chris and he chatted about members of the Jamaican family I didn't even know. They laughed about a TV show I didn't watch, his father never once mentioning the case or the charge or the possible outcomes. I found myself joining in some of the laughter but also feeling shocked by the casualness of his tone. As if it wasn't the end of the world for Chris. As if he didn't know what his life would be like if he was found guilty. As if it mattered if he really had done those things. I watched them both. It had been a long time since I'd sat so close to Chris's father. I was suddenly aware how alike they were, with sudden swings in mood. But I felt a strange pain too, as despite myself, I remembered happy times when Chris was small - the parties we used to give, friends and relatives round a table, groaning with food and drink.

Outside there was a bright, blue sky, the clean smell of frost, branches dazzling with sunlight on ice.

'Julie, let me take you for a meal. No reason to be enemies now. The boy need us both.'

He took my hand and, thinking he'd gone into automatic flirting mode, I pulled away.

'Have you got time from your other offspring?'

'Saint I'm not. You did a good job as a mother, boy, all those exams! You mustn't worry yourself too much. He got to live with his mistakes. I made mistakes too. I made a mistake in the way I treated you.'

Into my head, uninvited, comes the scene of our first meeting at the garage where I'd brought my car to be serviced. He invited me to visit his favourite sister and eat Jamaican food. She had put music on and we'd danced. I remembered the shirt he'd been wearing, black cotton with scarlet inserts. The sunlight picked out the grey strands in his hair.

Look what life turns you into if you're not careful. You learn to count the wrongs and nurse them, feed them with your own compost. All I ever wanted was intimacy and trust. And I thought I had that with my son. I thought we talked about everything and I thought I had tamed his father's wildness out of him. One tear slipped out the side of my eye and I quickly wiped it away.

'Ok. A meal.'

'We'll talk this through Julie. He need a lawyer on the ball. Get him a softer sentence.'

'He was there. He got involved.'

'I know. I know about wildness. Maybe he need to go home.'

'Home?'

'To the country. My cousins in Port Antonio, far from Kingston. They still there living the simple, good, clean life. Up at dawn, fishing, farming, to the market, Church on Sundays.'

'Then why aren't you like that?'

We were both pulling our coats tighter to our bodies in the cold. I put my hands deep in my pockets. I still felt drawn to him, still found him attractive but the cold stone of how he treated me lay on my tongue.

'You were very jealous. And possessive also, too much of Chris. It drive people away.'

I felt I would choke on the cold stone. My hands tightened in my pockets.

'Let him fly Julie. He making a mess I know but maybe he come back – and come back stronger.'

We sat side by side in court. One of Chris's so-called friends testified that it was Chris who produced the knife that was used to threaten the Pakistani shop-keeper, the knife that had never been found. Mr. Khan saw a knife wave in front of his face but wasn't sure where it came from. I imagined the gloom of the corner shop, lit by dull bulbs, the stacked up boxes blocking the light, the later hour, the dirty windows, the tired man about to lock up, wiping his hands on his overalls. I became rigid and felt Winfield turn to look at me, to see what was wrong. Chris's solicitor ran his hands through grey hair that was left too long, before he stood to question the other gang members. I noticed a gravy stain on the front of his gown. He offered Chris's plea of guilty to robbery but not guilty to threatening with a knife. The counsel for the prosecution asked Ste, one of Chris's so-called friends, what they had done with the money. He described a night of clubbing and cocaine, a party that ended up in the morning, lying on sand-dunes on the beach.

Winfield came back with me to the house. He went straight out the back to smoke and I followed with two mugs of tea and leaned against the back wall, warming my hands on the curve of the mug, decorated with images of Paris.

'Look like he get time Julie.' He touched the arm of my coat as he spoke.

I nodded. 'But maybe not for long and afterwards he could go to Port Antonio as you say. I don't think they can prove he held the knife. The jury might not believe that.'

He dropped the cigarette on the path and crushed it with his shoe. 'When he come out, he can work with me. Train as a mechanic. I know that not what you want, that you think he'll be a teacher or something one day, but it too late for that now.'

His padded, winter coat made his shoulders look wide so I leaned my head against one, some need for comfort, I guess. He stroked my head and said. 'I know Julie. I know what you've done. Any mother would have done the same. But now you got to back off. Get on with your own life.'

He had to get back. There was a business to run and I knew there were other children at home but I also knew that Chris was his first born and he wouldn't walk away now, like he had before. That he would do what he could to make things right for his son and that, in his own way, that was for me too.

Light Work

Kelly kicked off her shoes as she came home, the breeze off the Thames blowing her fine, wool skirt prettily. The house vibrated with Polish jazz tumbling in through the open French doors. Mick lay sprawled, covered with a sleeping bag, on a recliner in the back garden, a Red Stripe to his lips enjoying the first sunshine of spring. After he'd swallowed he said 'Hey there hun, how did it go?'

She leaned against the door frame and sighed. 'Did you read the letter from the clinic?' He took another swig. 'More time Kelly, more time.'

She pulled a brightly-coloured flyer out of her shoulder bag and threw it, so it landed on him. She poured herself a glass of Sauvignon from a bottle in the fridge and went out to sit on the edge of the recliner.

'You've never been to Romania have you? My father used to do a lot of business there. I've always wanted to go.'

Mick squinted through his sunglasses at the flyer, colour images of snow-capped mountains, thick forests, a bear and a gypsy band in a restaurant.

'I've got two weeks of holiday time. There's a Blues festival at a town called Sighisoara, all kinds of music - Eastern European blues, Fado, Rembetika, folk jazz. We could stop at Budapest on the way.'

'Drive? That's a hell of a way, hun. You up for that? I don't know much about the place apart from Dracula and orphans.'

'There's more to it than that Mick! You'd love the music, something new for you to feed off.' She pulled the clip out of her hair so that its brown strands fell silkily over her shoulders.

'But the clinic,' he said, frowning.

She closed her eyes; in fact she was blinking back tears. He reached for her hand.

Late that night, while he was out on a gig with the band, she pulled the blinds down in the bedroom, so the flashing lights from Canary Wharf wouldn't disturb her. Before switching off the computer she had one last look through the virtual rooms of the restaurant she was designing and went to bed. Half asleep, she rubbed the scar on her stomach, left when they'd removed the cyst.

As she got ready for work, Mick lay asleep, snoring lightly. She walked to the station, passing streams of children on their way to school. There were kids everywhere. All her friends had kids, toddlers, primary school children, teenagers, creamy ones, brown ones, freckled ones, blonde ones, curly-headed ones who they fussed over and spoiled and talked about endlessly. Her free hand clenched into a fist at the thought.

Everyone at the meeting loved the designs, darling, so airy and light and yet romantic. She fingered the small wooden cross around her neck for luck as the negotiations spun around some modifications and costs. Her fee would be paid in by the end of the week. They'd be able to afford a trip to Romania. Mick seemed to be getting bored by her need for a baby, the endless tears, the programmes, the meals and food intended to boost fertility, the operation, the drugs, the tests, the visits to the clinic. She was nearly forty and Mick was only thirty three and she thought, on the train back to the Island, about his lack of a sense of urgency. Sure, he'd love to have a miniature guitarist just like himself but she wanted a family, at least two children, with a mum and a dad, faces around the table at birthdays, family holidays playing cricket on a beach. All the things she'd never had. Mick had grown up with four siblings and spoke about the chaos, of having your special stuff borrowed by the others, of not having your own space, of the constant arguing and jostling for position. He wasn't bothered about replicating all that. 'Kelly,' he'd say. 'We're fine. We enjoy life, have our freedom. It's good.' And he'd hold her in his arms, his body against her back, his chin against the fine shreds of her hair, as she'd sob with yet more disappointment. 'It's not as if I want to be some kind of patriarch creating a wider tribe of Murphys, all with mops of thick, black hair and hazel eyes.' And so they'd fall asleep despite a helicopter overhead, shining its light into the recesses of the bad estate only a stone's throw away, looking for child tearaways. Or perhaps they would hear the faint throb of a disco boat on the Thames.

* * *

It's magical, like going back in time, thought Kelly, as the Renault finally crossed over the border into Romania. They passed another cart and mule and Kelly waved at the women in flowery dresses in the cart, one was breastfeeding a baby. Up the slopes of the hills, thick green forests formed a backdrop to small towns and villages. They were getting along better, en route, than they had for several years. They had to negotiate hotels, pensions and restaurants across Europe, struggling with menus they didn't understand, learning to enjoy polenta. They fell laughing onto the feather-filled duvet on their first night in Romania, when they discovered they'd eaten bear meat and Mick mimicked bear growls as he gnawed up the length of her slim white arms and along the satin skin of her shoulders, biting into her ankh tattoo. Afterwards, when she lay in bed wondering should she go and wash in the shower, where she'd seen cockroaches earlier, she was smiling, wondering if this might have worked because they had been so joyous, so delighted in each other, so much time to give each other and couldn't that just make the magic happen?

They bought pears from a market stall, pears soft as marshmallows and spat the pips out the car window as they drove. In a café, a local musician invited Mick to jam with them. He pushed his sunglasses onto the bandana, tying back his thick hair, to concentrate on the melody and rhythms as the violin ripped along. Kelly's cat-like face lit up with a smile at the fairy-tale nostalgia of it all, how the villages, with their onion-domed churches, reminded her of Chagall paintings.

All it needed was a flying horse or bride floating in the sky. They stopped to visit an old wooden church. She whipped off his bandana before they went in, using it as a shawl to cover the ankh tattoo on her shoulder. The cantor and the priest's chanting echoed almost hypnotically and they breathed in frankincense. The silver and gold icons glittered in the shadowed light and Kelly lit a thin, ochre candle, as she saw the other women do, and pushed it into the sand tray. Mick pointed to the wooden crosses for sale near the door, just like the one she always wore. She held her own, tightly, wishing, the only kind of prayer she knew, as her mother had never taken her to a church service or said a prayer with her. It was a foreign world and this was its most exotic manifestation. She found it both ridiculous and emotional, as if there was a part of her that wanted to believe that there was another level of being, a world of spirits and a God who might be entreated, might be watching over human life. She looked at Mick who had known all that, had known what it was to be brought up believing and seemed relaxed and at home in this incense-filled interior, with its press of women. She almost told him then. He seemed less edgy during this holiday, less likely to have a temper outburst but then he wasn't taking any stuff, anything that might be passed his way during the nights he worked with the band.

When they arrived in Sighisoara, they booked into the hotel and, over tea, read through the festival programme, ticking the events they wanted to see. She bent over to tie the laces on her boots as she said 'I think I might visit an orphanage while I'm here. I'll miss the Ukrainian night so I can take the babies' clothes, kids' games, medicines and stuff to the orphanage.'

Mick took off his sunglasses to look at her, for once his hazel eyes open, rather than sleepily half closed. 'What?'

'That second bag in the boot is full of gifts for an orphanage.' She carried on tying the intricate lacing on the other foot. Mick unzipped the guitar case and slipped the strap over his head.

'Kelly, what's this about?' He sat down and plucked at the strings, tuning up.

'I'm doing good works. Creating good karma.'

He carried on strumming, looking at her, but saying nothing.

The audience was a kaleidoscope of European nationalities, listening to a group of Bulgarian throat singers delivering what sounded like a lamentation. Its tone was ethereal, as if it wasn't human voices singing but some ancient sound bubbling up from underground the earth. She watched Mick out of the side of her eye and saw that intrigued look he got when he heard new kinds of music.

'Epic,' he said.

It shifted her mood. They went for a drink in a club in Citadel Square and he dropped down beside her with two beers.

'Did you say your father used to do business here? What kind of business?'

The cold beer stung her throat. 'Well, as far as I know and, remember I didn't see him that often, it was something to do with furs, bringing furs back to UK.'

He giggled. 'Not bear fur?'

'Yes, I suppose, and wolf, fox, beaver? Whatever.'

The corners of his eyes crinkled with amusement. 'Nice.'

'We ate bear two days ago, Mick.'

'Yeah hun, by mistake if I remember. Let me ask you something Kelly. This baby thing is about him isn't it? You never had a real Dad.'

'Just Mum and me. Occasional visits. I've got a half-sister, apparently.'

He put his arm around her shoulder. 'Well, I've got enough nieces and nephews now for a football team. You know I'm not that bothered about bringing more children into this shitty world.'

She put one finger on his lips. He didn't understand what she was feeling, this ache of not being fully human. She knew her body was telling her that time was running out, that her body, everyone's body was subject to time, that the body was not eternal, that the limits were fixed, immutable. She knew her mother regretted having such a tiny family. She sprinkled bitterness into her gin, bitterness at her bad decisions and the long and painful consequences. She shivered for a second, thinking of her mother, living alone and longing for grandchildren.

'Cold, hun?' He took off his leather jacket and put it around her shoulders.

'We're good together Mick, aren't we? You're with me on everything I do?'

He turned his head to look at her.

The hotel called her a taxi in the morning and the fat driver didn't seem surprised when she asked him to take her to the orphanage. She noticed that his eyes flicked to her on and off in the rear view mirror and she pulled her jacket across her sweatshirt. She asked him to open the window because of his cigarette smoke and attempted small talk about the festival but his English was limited. At a busy junction he turned around and said 'Baby?'

She stopped breathing. Was it that obvious? How come Mick hadn't read what was written across her forehead? The doors to the orphanage were opened by a young woman with black hair, tied in plaits around her head. This emphasised the soft roundness of her face, the enormous, brown eyes and the dark down on her upper lip. Kelly followed her down the corridor, noticing the limp and the curvy shape of her body. The kitchen smelt of onions and sour milk. Together, under the dim lights, they opened the packages of calpol and cough mixture, the parcels of baby clothes. She told the young woman her name and she replied with 'Crista. My name is Crista.'

All her features seemed dramatic, thought Kelly, as if she was heavily made-up, when she was wearing no make-up at all. It made her feel faded as an old watercolour.

'You like to see the children?' asked Crista, as she held up a couple of toddlers' dresses, smoothing the flower-patterned cotton.

The dormitories smelt of urine. She noticed how cold the rooms seemed and wondered if this was the reason why the babies and toddlers were wearing knitted woollen jump suits and hats. Some of the toddlers pulled themselves up by the railings on the cot to stare at them. One little girl held up a small soft giraffe, another a plastic black baby. In the crying and shouting, Kelly dug her nails into the palm of her hand to fight back tears. She stopped by one baby girl with blonde curls and green eyes, patting her head and pinching her cheek. Crista pulled her into another room where dozens of bunk-beds were stacked. The beds were neatly made.

'Children gone school,' said Crista.

'And these?' gestured Kelly.

Crista pointed to one boy of about eight and mimed that he was blind, to another with a hunchback. Kelly, brought face to face with so much suffering, was frightened, finding herself outside the parameters of her own prosperous world. True she hadn't grown up with a father but her mother had made sure she'd been safe and loved.

'Government stop adoption,' said Crista, turning to look

at her with those large, conker coloured eyes.

Kelly shook her head. 'I didn't know that.'

At the Al Cook event, Mick was on familiar ground and had chatted to some of the backing musicians before the show, wangling an invitation to the late night party. He told Kelly about it over a beer. She made her excuses. She needed time think and, if she went, they'd both get wasted and she wasn't in the mood. He put his arm around her as they walked back to the hotel, her heels clattering on the cobbled roads. As Mick opened the glass door, a figure came out of the shadows. She touched Kelly on the arm, whispering that she could help her.

'Not now.' Kelly turned to Crista, frowning. 'Tomorrow at ten in the morning.'

'What's going on?' Mick loomed over them with beery breath.

In the lift he stroked the side of her face with his calloused fingers and said 'What?'

She told him about the visit to the orphanage, and that Crista had wanted to thank her for all the gifts and wanted to see her, probably to find out if there was more help, maybe money, but by the end of the explanation Mick had ceased listening. He ran his fingers through his hair and packed his guitar into the case to take to the party.

Crista wouldn't come inside the hotel for a coffee, so they walked through the narrow streets of Baroque apricot and white buildings, leaving the tourist areas and stopped at a cafe. Kelly again noticed how beautiful the woman was. She pointed to the wooden cross she was wearing and pulled out her own, on a silver chain, from under her sweater. Crista smiled

'You, Orthodox?'

Kelly just shook her head. It was too complicated to explain.

'You want baby?' The question came out under the hubbub of the cafe. She nodded. What use was it pretending? The woman's gaze was so intense, she flinched.

'I am child of orphanage. Better for baby to have mother. I know that. Now only way is to buy baby.'

'What? Pay the orphanage?'

'Perhaps. But I know woman. She has too many children. She will put this baby in orphanage.'

While this information sank in, Kelly asked her about her life and, in her limited vocabulary, Crista told her about the polio, about how she was left in the orphanage, how sad life had been but now things had got better but still, and how she wanted to be a nun but now she could not. Kelly wanted to ask why, but something about the sadness of her expression prevented her. As Kelly was putting her purse away after paying the bill, Crista looked at her and said.

'You will need $12,000.'

Kelly breathed in to control her shock. 'She's selling her

baby for $12000?'

'It cost that here. More if you go through orphanage.'

'I'm not rich. It would take me a year to find that kind of cash. But I would love the baby, give him or her a happy home.'

'It is poverty that makes people bad. She thinks she find a rich American.'

When she got back to the hotel Mick was in bed, still sleeping with the TV on. She woke him and they decided to be tourists for the day, making a visit to Dracula's house. Mick enjoyed the ghoulish connotations of the venue but soon got bored with the history. Kelly's mind was in a whirl of doubts and calculations. How much could she get out of cash machines in three days? Maybe £900 or £1000. And where would the rest come from? There was a fever of recklessness inside her. I must see the baby, she thought, yes, see the baby and then make a decision. They had lunch in the restaurant and Mick lifted his glass

'I like it here hun. Nice people. Relaxed. Don't see any protests about English coming on holiday, not like all the shit in the papers about Romanians coming to England.'

Would you like a Romanian baby, she thought, Oh Mick, I should tell you but she knew he'd try to stop her even going to look at the baby, if she did.

Crista and Kelly took a taxi to the outskirts of the city, well beyond the picturesque streets and medieval towers. It was an estate of concrete blocks of flats, without trees or green spaces. Rubbish blew around the yards they crossed, where teenage boys hung around smoking, a group inside and leaning against a wrecked Skoda without wheels, watching them. Two locks were turned to open the steel door into the flat. A toddler in a nappy was sat in the corridor on torn Lino and a five year old was feeding her from a plastic dish. The mother, in a long skirt, patterned in purple and red flowers, was holding the baby, wrapped in a small blanket. A man with dark olive skin, wearing a trilby, was smoking in a chair. The mother turned to look at Kelly, up and down. The patterned scarf she was wearing was tied round and under a long plait. She was stout and smelt of sweat and garlic. Crista lifted the baby from the mother's arms and held him out to Kelly.

'Luca. His name is Luca. He is six months.'

His huge dark eyes focussed on Kelly's face. His ears stuck out from the side of his head and his black hair grew in spiky tufts. She reached to touch his hand and his fingers took hold of her finger. Crista pushed him into her arms and she held him up facing her. He seemed so placid, so unbothered by being passed from person to person. He felt light. She could feel her heart beating faster and an excited glow of love, that this baby could be hers, if only. He made a stream of noises like water gurgling over rocks and she wondered what he was trying to say.

Crista touched her on the arm. 'She has too many children. She cannot keep this one. Husband not working.' She pointed to the man in the trilby hat, smoking and examining her.

'Twelve thousand dollars,' he said.

Luca reached for her silver chain that was catching the light from the bare bulb overhead. He pulled the wooden cross into his mouth.

'I can't find that money just now - give me time.'

She got out of the taxi at the edge of the tourist area and walked through the cold dusk, jamming her hands into the pockets of her suede jacket. There was a kind of madness in her, a frantic insistence that she must do this, now or never. Mick wasn't in the room but had left a note. In the bathroom she noticed that she had not become pregnant through the happy lovemaking of their holiday. She cleaned herself up and headed to the club, stopping to withdraw her first wad of notes, checking them against the exchange calculator. The next evening she did the same and during the day phoned her mother, asking her to send cash by money gram. She felt nervous around Mick. Surely he would notice her feverish tension. Over their lunch of soup he told her she was like a cat on hot bricks.

'Just the time of the month,' she said, stirring the thin liquid.

He came home in the early hours of the morning, after yet another party. She knew from his eyes he'd been taking something. So much for his promises. She went through his wallet and took out another wad of cash. As he lay there in a deep sleep, she watched him, gone, his dark hair falling over his face, his mouth dribbling.

'I'm sorry. I have to.'

She picked up his guitar, his Fender acoustic, the love of his life, in its dark blue case and left the hotel. In the main music venue she cello-taped a for sale sign to it, $3000.

Early evening she phoned Crista to tell her she had half the money and to ask about the documents and the practicalities of the adoption. The consequences of what love was driving her to do were becoming clearer. Crista told her about a local lawyer who arranged things for the orphanage and would act for her too, for a fee.

'Ask them if they will take half now and then the rest when the legalities are sorted.'

Crista agreed but told her that she didn't think they would hand over the baby until the money was paid. They travelled to the block of flats again. Luca was asleep in his cot, in a room full of cigarette smoke and steam from a stew cooking in the kitchen. Kelly sat down while Crista and the mother talked. The mother's tone was agitated but Crista seemed to calm her down and she passed Kelly the sleeping baby, the body against hers burning with heat. She desperately wanted to leave this chaotic place, this scene of her own desperation. Crista had a letter of agreement for the mother to sign.

'She says you can keep the baby, here in Sighisoara, until you pay the rest of the money. Then you go back to your country with him. She says her people watch you. They know where you go.'

The menace hidden in the words was not lost on Kelly. She gathered the bag of clothes the mother had prepared. The mother held up one breast through her clothes and pointed at Luca. Crista told her she should buy baby milk and a bottle on the way back to the hotel. I'll need to get nappies and wipes too, Kelly thought, going over memories of helping her friends with their new babies.

The mother picked up Luca and murmured over him. Was she praying in her own language, Kelly wondered. She was moved by this moment of tenderness and she hesitated for a moment, as Crista gathered up documents and belongings. What was she doing? Was this right? She saw the mother split off some of the notes and pass them to Crista, who slipped them into the pocket of her trousers. In the taxi back to the hotel Kelly couldn't stop crying. Deep sobs welled up from her gut as she looked at the face of the sleeping baby, his long, black eyelashes casting shadows over his cheeks, the dirty dummy in his mouth.

'What is the matter?' Crista put her hand on hers but Kelly could say nothing.

The hotel receptionist looked up, surprised, when she walked through the foyer carrying a sleeping baby and helped her put the bags in the lift. The low sun of dusk was streaming through the windows of their room. Mick was sprawled out in his boxers, a cup of coffee gone cold beside him. He struggled to wake and then opened his eyes wide when he saw Kelly.

'Where the fuck have you been all day, hun?' he stared at the bundle in her arms. 'And what is that?'

'This is Luca.' She sat on the end of the bed and slipped the bag of clothes off her shoulder. 'He needs some nappies and baby milk. I'll have to ask reception where I can get them before he wakes up.'

'What have you done?' They sat silently looking at each other. She lay the baby down on the bed, so carefully, as if he was made of glass.

'Kelly.'

'You know what I've done. Luca is mine now. His mother doesn't want him. She has too many children.'

He stood by the window, the sunlight catching threads of auburn in his hair. 'But you never even told me.' He shook his head. 'And where's my fucking Fender?'

'You buy babies here. It's expensive.'

He slammed his fist against the wall and rested his head against the window. Kelly reached for her wooden cross, holding it, wishing.

'You're fucking nuts. This whole baby think has made you crazy. You've got to give the baby back.'

'He's mine, to love and care for. It's what I want Mick. Please say you'll be with me on this. A son. A gorgeous, little boy to be a part of our life. I'll buy you another guitar. I'm sorry about that.'

He sat down on the bed and looked at her and Luca.

'But he's not mine, Kelly. We don't know anything about the people he comes from. Is he a gypsy baby? How do you know whether there isn't something wrong with him? This is madness. You take him back to the mother and let's go home and get on with our lives, otherwise, there might be no 'us' anymore.'

She shook her small cat-shaped head and somehow, from somewhere deep inside, a resolution kicked in, a sense of need and determination so she turned to him.

'I'm staying here to sort out the papers and raise the rest of the money. You go back if you want.' She reached over for his hand but he pulled it away. 'I love you Mick, but you don't want to share this with me. You don't get what I'm feeling. Throat singers digging into their souls, you get that. But pretty Kelly with her kitten heels and stylish restaurants, you don't really see me.'

She watched him pack his things and she knew this might be an ending. She sighed, thinking of all the complications but, mostly, watching the shape of his familiar body, as he turned and swivelled from one cupboard to another, collecting bits of paper and CDs scattered over the floor. The baby was stirring, waving his fists in the air. There were more important things to see to.

Snow on Snow

When he hears the Jamaican accent through the phone, his face tightens. It usually means his father wants something. His eyes half close as he weighs up the truth. He notices how his father's voice sounds, like a tenor singer. All sweetness. It's dusk and the sodium streetlights have come on, which he can see through the sitting room window. Snowflakes pattern down through the yellowing light. The rooftops of the houses opposite have been iced with a thin layer of snow.

'Damn cold Leo. Rass claat'

'What about a rescue service? The police patrol will stop and help get a garage out to tow you.'

'You think Babylon goin' to rescue an old black man? Anyway, ain't got no cash.'

Don't, thinks Leo, Don't pull the you've got to help me because this country's racist card from the pack. You've done it too often. He excuses himself and says he'll call back when he's seen to the kids.

'Lend me a tenner Leo'. As Gemma bends over to zip up her high-heeled boots her red hair falls into her mouth. 'I'm going to the offie – need a Chardonnay.'

Leo gets his wallet out, flicking open the buttery leather flap. As he pulls out a note he snags something under Milly and Jake's photo. It's a tattered snap of himself as a four year old with a fuzz of dandelion hair, leaning against his Dad who looks cool in a jaunty velvet cap.

'Daddy.' There's a wail from upstairs and another one.

'There's a sad dog.'

'It's your turn,' says Gemma.

'While you satisfy your alkie cravings?'

'I was not the adult being summoned.'

'The football's about to start.'

'I'm out of here.' As she opens the front door, a blast of snowflakes float in, melting into spots of water on the carpet.

'Daddy!' The voices are getting screamier. He takes the stairs two at a time. Milly stands on her princess pillows and points through the clotted flakes on the window.

'Doggie's lost in the snow. Look Daddy.'

'Lost. Lost,' adds Jake.

Lamplight in the street glimmers amber through the gauze of falling snow. There are slight indentations where people have walked. A stout black dog looks up to the lit window. The snow forms a crust on his fur. His stance suggests middle age and he's of no discernible breed.

'He's so cold Daddy.' Milly looks up to her father with tragic brown eyes.

'He'll make a mess on the carpet.' The children start wailing.

'Your mum'll be furious.'

'Baby Jesus loves him,' says Milly.

Leo looks at his watch and thinks his own mother, now she's born-again, has a lot to answer for. Two minutes to kick off. 'O.K. Just let him in for a few minutes to warm up, then but after he'll have to go home.'

The children jump down from their beds and follow Daddy downstairs. Leo opens the front door and a blast of snow hits him. He tastes some on his tongue as he shouts the dog over.

The dog waddles into the sitting room and sinks in front of the gas fire, shivering. Leo looks for an old tea towel and rubs its back. Milly and Jake stand close to the dog staring at it. The dog lifts his heavy black head and sad, slow eyes.

'Now I have to explain this to your mother,' he says. He lifts one child under each arm and runs upstairs as they giggle and throws them laughing onto their beds.

'Now then.' He puts his hands on both hips 'Sleep time. Daddy's going to watch Man U.' He jumps and does a mock header at the light shade and flees downstairs just as the telephone rings again. He can hear Gemma turning her key in the lock and the scrape of sole on welcome mat.

'Yeah Dad. I'm still here. It's frigging snowing like the end of the world. Haven't you found anyone to rescue you yet?' He can hear the pop of a cork from the kitchen.

'I told you already. It would take me 4 hours to get down to that bit of the M1 in this weather. It's two days before

Christmas. Gemma won't want me going away.' Pause. 'Suddenly you're my father are you?'

Gemma walks in with two glasses of wine. She stands still, listening to the conversation and taking in the large, wet dog before the fire. Her eyebrows lift like a bridge about to let through an oil tanker. Leo puts down the phone.

'Why isn't he in the AA or something?'

'Cos he's a pillock. Something useful like car rescue doesn't take precedence over the bookie's.'

She wrinkles her nose as the smell of wet dog hits her. He points out the soft heartedness of the children and their distress at seeing it lost in the snow.

'When the snow stops it can find its way home,' he says, his eyes focused on the TV screen where the match has started. She unzips her boots and settles on the settee, her back stiff with annoyance, but noticing the crinkled photo on the floor, she picks it up and hands it to Leo with the change from the tenner. The dog watches her face warily. They can hear the wind against the windows and its whine as it flicks round the corner of the house. There's a soft thud of falling flakes against the glass and an immense silence presses against the walls of the house, as if it had suddenly been lifted from its street and sent spiralling out into the cold and still universe.

*   *   *

Two hundred and fifty miles away Eric sits hunched in his beat up Datsun. He's pulled a blanket round his shoulder and the red ring of a cigarette shines through the misting up windscreen. Snow begins to pack into the corners of the car windows in soft triangles. He feels the ice begin to lick his feet. The peak of his cap hangs over his dark, lined face and the small brilliant eyes are deep in their sockets. There is no street lighting so the snow's whiteness lights up the undulating fields. Eric unwinds the car window and throws out the cigarette butt. A blast of freezing air fills the car and he shivers and curses the night and his rotten life.

*   *   *

As the room fills with roars from the football, a small brown head with a halo of soft curls slides round the edge of the door.

'What are you doing out of bed?' asks Gemma. The baubles from the Christmas tree reflect in the curve of her wine glass.

'This is my best pillow for the sad dog. And can I take him to see the crib, the animals and baby Jesus?' The princess pillow is trailing behind her. The dog lifts its heavy head. Its red tongue lolls out now that it's warmed up. As if summoned by its own princess, it gets up and pads across to the little girl. The spotlights in the football ground illuminate a flurry of snowflakes falling on the scramble of players.

'Looks like the game will be called off,' says Leo and follows the dog and Milly along the corridor into the dining room, where a crib of shiny wooden figures is assembled on the windowsill, an African faced Mary. Joseph in a loose agbada stands behind her.

'Jesus will keep you safe. Godbless.' Milly joins her hands together and closes her eyes. 'Amen,' says Leo. Milly then starts another longer prayer she's learned from Grandma. 'We thank you for the world we have, we thank you....'

'Time for bed, princess. The dog's safe but tomorrow he'll have to go home, home to his own family for Christmas.'

'But Dad..'

A gauze curtain of snow hangs over the windows. It casts an eerie light on the figures so that the wooden baby shimmers in the reflection.

There were no carpets but the Christmas tree was covered in lights of different colours. The red ones cast a pink glow on his mother's cheeks, where she kneeled in the corner of the room. His father filled the frame of the doorway, smoke billowing before him like incense. He seemed to glide over the floor and stand over his mother. She was sobbing. His father had his hands round her throat.

'Don't you ever... don't you ever be checking up on me like that ... you stupid bitch.'

He remembered freezing in the room, though the gas fire must have been on full blast. His father let go his mother's throat and spun round to pickup Leo by the back of his sweater.

'So you tell your mammy where we go ugh? I not tell you

be quiet Leo? I not tell you what gwine happen if you say?'

He remembered swinging from the fist that gripped the fold of his red sweater, as he was carried down the hallway and thrown into the cupboard under the stairs. He fell against a pile of shoes and rubbery Wellingtons, into the dark and cold of his Christmas. He thought if he sat very still the bad things would stop but he heard his mammy screaming and put his hands over his ears. The door of the cupboard jerked open and yellow light spilt onto his upturned face. His father had the space station, Santa Claus had brought. His father snapped off the canopy and threw it over his shoulder. Then he snapped off the petrol pumps that filled the rockets and threw the broken toy into the darkness of the cupboard.

He carries Milly up to bed, tucking her in like a sausage roll, just as his mother used to do and kisses her on the forehead.

'Baby Jesus thinks you are very kind Daddy.'

'I know petal, I know.' When he gets down to the hallway he slips his padded coat on and his feet into unlaced trainers.

'Gemma. I've got to. This weather – he might freeze to death.'

'He's never done anything for you Leo and it's two days before Christmas and the roads will be so dangerous.'

'No they'll grit the motorways clear. It's OK. I know what he is but I can't, I just can't leave him out there.'

'You soft lad.' She looks up at him. He can see melted

snowflakes sliding down her long silky hair. 'And what in God's name am I supposed to do with this mutt in the morning, when you won't be back?'

As he steps out into the street a blast of icy wind shouts into the house. Both the dog and Gemma edge closer to the fire.

*   *   *

It is darkening. The mauve clouds are strips of ribbon, patterned against pale lemon. The trees are silhouetted like skeletons against this fading light. Across the snow, Eric can see the windows of a farmhouse, tiny orange squares of light. He can make out a column of smoke from the chimney. He takes another shirt out of his bag and puts it on under his jumper, and another pair of socks. 'Leo gwine come for me. I spend more time with him than any of the other pikney.' He takes out a cigarette and a small packet of grass and rolls a spliff. Its incense fills the car with its liturgical atmosphere. He feels the vibration of the phone in his pocket and answers, listening to Leo tell him that he's just set off.

'About damn time. You wan me freeze to death Leo?'

He steps out into the snow, surprised by how deep it is, already up to his knees. He knocks snow off the windscreen with his elbow and flicks the wipers. The cold wind blows the storm horizontally into his face, so that frozen particles settle on his eyelashes and moustache. He jumps up and down and hits his body with his fists to get the circulation going. The last of the light is deepening into dark grey. He looks at the angles and dents of the flattened landscape, how it refracts the last strips of yellow and purple sky, how all the filth of mud and stubble and manure are re-baptized by the pure coldness.

Suddenly a memory returns of how excited he was as a boy of ten when he first saw snow. He and his brothers ran into the streets of Paddington and stuck out their tongues to catch snow flakes and taste them.

He picks up a handful of snow and puts it to his mouth – fresh and clean, like mountain water. The wind seems to be picking up speed and the rhythmic brush and sigh as the trees bend and release reminds him of the surf against the rocks of the beach back home.

The cold is burning his face so he gets back into the car, pulls another shirt over him and releases the back of the chair. Although he is shivering, he feels an immense desire to sleep, to forget the failures, the unpaid debts, the evictions, the resentful children and list of women who will never forgive him. 'What they expect? I not that bad – a man got to survive in Babylon. The pressure,' he mutters. 'The pressure.'. He drifts off into a cold, deep, unbreakable sleep.

The Sea-Coloured Gown

The train trembled into movement before I scrambled into the only empty seat, next to a man who looked like a trimmer version of Mugabe, with the tache under the nose. A hundred miles of waterlogged farmland slid past as I flicked through my book.

I leaned against the dirty window and thought about my children, their hormones like electric impulses charging through the void. I also thought about loneliness – about stress and work and lying awake at night, drinking it in. As I did so the book slid to the floor and he gallantly reached for it under the seat, handing it over.

'Is it a good novel?' He was looking at the cover of *Say You're One of Them*.

'I like stories set in countries I can travel to in my mind but can't in real life but this one is very grim about the lives of children in different African countries.'

'Usually grim, the news here, about Africa.'

'Oh.' I didn't know what to say, thinking I'd been not very PC, or even God forbid, racist. I'd been trained in cultural differences so I knew about those things. I apologised for disturbing him while I went to get a sandwich. I squeezed back into my seat.

'I hope you don't mind, I've been flicking through your

book to see if there were any stories set in Zimbabwe.' He handed the book back to me.

'No problem. Is that where you're from?'

'It is. I'm here doing a PhD at Edinburgh. Veterinary studies.'

'Oh. I like animals,' I said, thinking we might pass the time with an interesting topic of conversation. He explained he was looking at the psychology of stressed turkeys in factory farms, so we talked about happy meat and the price of food and went on from there to weird and wonderful animal facts. I was amazed how much I remembered from projects the kids had done in primary school and I got onto elephants. 'I really love elephants. They bury their dead you know.'

Despite the thick glasses, I could tell he was sceptical. I was curious to know what he thought about Mugabe, especially when he had the same kind of style. After all, it had been on the news, impossible to ignore. I listened, in and out, as you do when the subject is arcane, to his justification of farm take-overs. This was nice, I thought, having a conversation with a man outside work and I felt myself getting just a bit flirty.

When we got to London he slid out a business card and asked for mine but I laughed and told him Darlington social services didn't do cards.

Months passed and nothing from the man in the train with the neat moustache but over a coffee, I'd think would a man fancy me again? Fat and over forty? Arsey teenage children.

At Christmas I sent a card. A month later there was an e mail:

Nice to hear from you. I've been home for months, unexpectedly. This has delayed thesis. Now back in Edinburgh.

So I tapped back about Christmas, the kids' piercings and the eating of stressed-out turkeys - making light of my exhaustion and the problems with the kids, Milly sat on the wall out front with a succession of fourteen year old boys. I looked in the magnifying mirror which Milly, so kindly, gave me as a present and my face was an ordinance survey map.

I've got a weekend free; why not get the train to Edinburgh for the day. You said you'd never been.

I thought about the expense of the ticket and anxiety about what might or might not happen. Milly came home from the school disco with love-bites on her neck. I was ironing with the news on. I needed to keep up to date with Zimbabwe. She flicked to Emmerdale.

'Put that back on the news!'

'You've always got the news on now. It's so last century.'

'I want to know what's happening in the world. And so should you.'

'The world's shot and you keep me in solitary confinement. It's not fair, why can't I go clubbing for Charlotte's fourteenth?' She threw herself across the settee.

'You're too young. Clubs are full of older, predatory men.' I slammed the iron down on pillow case.

'Predatory?' she mouthed the syllables as if she was eating a rotten banana.

As I slipped into bed that night, wearing my flannelette pyjamas, I noticed how cold the sheets were. I got out of bed to check my email and caught the image of my own face in the unlit, grey screen. Is this my life, I thought, running round after other people's tragedies, sorting out arguments, snatching moments for myself. Why shouldn't I have a date?

He looked nice in his corduroy trousers and tartan scarf. I'd squeezed into magic-knickers so I looked ok in my two-way stretch trousers. We climbed up all the steep steps and went for coffee and cake in Princess St. It was cold and windy so the café was full of Edinburgh's multi-lingual tourists and students.

'The research is going well – I'm focusing on cannibalism.'

'I can't afford to eat happy turkeys,' I said. 'Are you married?'

'Yes. We have five children.'

I bit into creamy topping. 'That's a lot of children to bring up. Does your wife work?'

'She's a teacher. We have help at home.'

Of course you would, I thought. He asked about my husband and I gave a brief summary of ten years of marriage but didn't tell him about the violence. I didn't want to sound like a victim. He didn't mention his wife again or make any cheesy comments about them not getting on, so I let it go.

It was a long walk to his flat through streets where the wind blew leaves and paper bags in a dance, up and over the pavements. He took my gloved hand and led me up the tenement stairs to where he'd prepared a peppery stew. On the mantelpiece there was a photograph of his children in front of a bungalow, surrounded by flame trees and I thought of my terraced house where the sitting-room carpet was badly-joined ends-of-rolls.

The stew made me sweat so the beer went down fast. We washed up together and bumped into each other in the kitchenette. I wondered if he could feel me tremble with so much longing and loneliness locked inside me. I knew I should pull on my coat and catch my train but I didn't because he stroked me and there were no bones left in my body. I was all liquid. After all the fumbling with buttons and zips we sort of fell into it in an unhurried way.

He walked me to the station. I was feeling light-headed and wondered what I was going to say to the kids.

'I like you Sally,' he held my hand and kissed me on the forehead. 'You know I'm only here for another six months, don't you?' I nodded. What else was there to say? I wanted to be sophisticated.

I went to Edinburgh many times. The daffodils bloomed and the swallows circled Arthur's Hill. I never used the word adultery. She was a thousand miles away. I took to getting Milly to colour my hair and she was surprisingly good at it. When I talked about some of the bad cases I worked on that troubled me, he listened. He told me about his struggles to get an education but there were gaps in his story. I wanted to eat his world, taste his childhood, his growing, and his cleverness.

There was this cut-off point for us that he'd told me about but which I'd forgotten. The book shelves in the flat were cleared and all the CDs packed away. It was physical this fear of him going, of abandonment, of loneliness.

'You know more about animals than about people,' I hissed. How I had hoped to be grown up when the time came.

'I told you I have to go back.'

'Couldn't you take me as a second wife? Build me a hut at the end of your garden? '

'We don't have second wives in Zimbabwe, we're Christians.'

'Jesus, what kind of Christian are you? I've neglected my children with all these visits.'

'Sally, I'm sorry. I don't want it to end badly. We had a nice time didn't we? You'll always have a special place in my heart.'

I collapsed into sobs against the wall and slid down to a squat.

'I have a present for you.'

It was an African gown with a pattern of swirling sea colours and turquoise embroidery around the neck.

'It's a gesture of my feelings towards you which are, unfortunately, circumscribed by our geography.'

I wanted to beat him up but my fists felt like lead.

'You, you've pecked out my heart and eaten it.'

The Queen of Sheba

The boredom gnawed at Suli. It was grey. The mist that rolled in off the North Sea sucked all the colour out. Sometimes the sun would burn it off and then the drab streets would brighten.

The colourful leaflet had caught his eye. 'The Hall's splendid and extraordinary gardens,' it said. When he first came to this town he'd admired the orderly gardens in front of the rows of identical houses. White and grey heads bent over to weed or dig in a seedling or tie up a row of spidery bean stalks.

The five-mile walk took him beyond the town. The hills rose in the distance and sun broke through the mist shining on the treeless hills, layered in strips of green. The slopes were dotted with sheep and a large hawk hung in the air over the highest hill.

An elderly couple walked past, hand in hand. 'Afternoon,' they said together.

'Pa,' he asked, waving the leaflet. 'Which is the road to the Hall?'

The red-faced man pointed in a diagonal direction, so Suli loped up the path. A rabbit rushed out of the hedge and disappeared into the field where a many-coloured bird with a long tail stood, poised. I could catch that, he thought.

He remembered going out with his uncle in the mountains behind Freetown, hunting for squirrel and monkey, which his aunt would later cook up in a tasty sauce.

There was an entrance fee for the garden and Suli counted out his precious cash. He told the receptionist that he was a student and had forgotten his card, so that he would get a reduction. She nodded him through.

In the first garden there were roses planted into thickets of colour, yellow then orange, then pink, then dark red. White roses grew all over the brick wall like stars in the night sky. He sat down on a bench and ate some bread but the scent of the roses made him almost dizzy. His mother would love this. She tried to grow flowers in empty food tins on the balcony of their flat.

He was amazed by the stunning colours of the next garden, surprised that such flowers could grow in a cold climate – spiky ones with rasta stripes, orange lilies, feathery pink blossoms. The next garden contained only plants that were poisonous, bushes with black or red berries, tall stalks with mauve flowers and others with pale yellow heads. People back home often claimed that a relative had been poisoned when there was a sudden death but he thought it was likely they couldn't afford a doctor. His uncle had told him about how, in the village, if a crocodile was killed, the chief had to be present when it was skinned and cut up because its gall was so deadly, it could be used as a poison.

He thought how good it would be to be here with a girl. Maybe if he brought back some flowers and gave them to the one who worked in the bar at the students' union, she would meet him. She had been kind, smiling and putting her finger on her lips when he said he didn't have the money to buy another drink and slipped him a beer. But would she really help him?

'Find a girl to marry you,' Claude had said. 'Lots of the guys have done it.'

He was cooking cows' feet in the hostel kitchen.

'If it that simple why are you to be deported?'

They ate licking the sauce off their fingers. They were trying to eat just once a day to make the money last.

'If I could get my stay I could study, become a lawyer. Back home I never finished my course. We ran out of money.'

As he cleared up the plates Claude said. 'Too rough here. In London it was better. I saw two girls drunk yesterday, staggering with small children. They looked cold and unhealthy.'

Suli washed up and went to his room to read his Bible. If I believe strong enough, he thought, God will help me.

The girl at the ticket desk didn't look up as he left, so she didn't see the leaves that stuck through the flap on the rucksack. He jogged a little on the long way back to town, shaking up the flowers in his bag so that he left a trail of essence of roses. It followed him into the hostel, mingling with the scent of onions and spices.

Suli gathered the roses in a pattern so a red one was next to a white, then a pink, then a yellow. He found a sheet of white paper and wrapped the bouquet. He put on a clean t-shirt he'd bought in a charity shop and checked his face to make sure there were no spots.

She was wiping the bar when he arrived, her brown hair scraped back into a spiky tail with strands down her neck. As always she wore a black t-shirt and jeans. He liked it that she didn't wear make up – just sometimes a little lipstick. I don't even know her name, he thought. The bar was nearly empty, just one couple sat in a dark corner. Some Kanye was playing on the juke-box and he matched his stride to the rhythm.

'Hey it's you again,' she looked up and smiled. 'How's it going?'

He placed the bouquet on the counter, an offering to whichever spirit was looking out for him.

'For you,' he spoke softly. 'I don't even know your name.'

'Charlotte – people call me Lottie. And you?'

'Suli. Well Suleiman for real. But you know.'

She held out her arms and gathered the roses to her face, breathing in the fragrance.

'They're so beautiful, like garden roses, not shop ones.' She smiled showing small teeth, a smile that set her eyes alight.

'Lottie, I would like to meet you after work. I like you.' He hoped he didn't sound too formal. It was difficult to know how these people did the courting thing – how much you said exactly, how much you hinted, how much you used eyes or hands. He thought her skin must be really soft, there was a sort of bloom on it, like on the rose petals. And now her cheeks had gone deep pink. She looked up at him – those eyes, pale like an afternoon sky. It was difficult to know what they were thinking.

'I finish at 6. It's Ok then but Suli you know I have a boyfriend.'

He wasn't sure what that meant. Was it a yes? Sometimes back home a girl might have several boyfriends. They helped her in various ways. The girls at Deeper Life Church didn't do that.

He waited outside by the tables where the smokers sat. He noticed some of the girls looking at him, a look that stayed for longer than a curious glance. I'm a good-looking man he thought but I really like this Charlotte. I wonder if she's a good girl. Maybe she's loose. He opened the small Bible he kept in his back pocket at random and read the story of Ruth.

She swung herself over the bench carrying her roses.

'Would you like something to eat? he asked. 'My friend Claude has cooked a hot pepper soup. Back at the hostel.' They walked along the grimy streets and he told her about his family and how he'd managed to get to England. She'd heard about the war, seen the news and the film 'Blood Diamonds'.

She told him about her course and about her divorced parents in Nottingham.

She fanned the heat away from her mouth as she ate. He poured her a glass of water from the tap and one for himself. People came in and out of the kitchen while they ate. A woman came in carrying a sleeping baby on her back. She washed up her dishes in silence without looking at Charlotte and left.

'It's like the United Nations in here,' she laughed. 'I had no idea people lived like this in this town.' She looked at her watch. 'It's eight. I'm sorry Suli I have to go, I have to meet my, er, boyfriend.'

He lifted her hand off the table. 'Stay, Lottie.' He rubbed her hand with his thumb. Her hand was soft. She hadn't done much hard work he thought. 'What does he do, this your boyfriend?'

'He works on the rigs in Aberdeen.'

Suli had a vague idea of what that might mean. 'I like you. Can we meet again?'

She pulled a strand of her hair into her mouth and sucked on it.

'I suppose we could do this again.'

He realised he wouldn't have enough money to take her out to a club but better to keep trying. When she left, he went next door to the Kebab shop where he washed up for four hours, earning two pounds an hour. As he scoured the trays with wire wool till the skin of his hands became grey and wrinkled, he worked out the dates in his head. His hearing was in four months' time. If they found against him, he would be told to leave the country, might be sent to a detention centre till he did. Like being in prison. The shame of it. He sang along with the music on the radio - My girl….

A week later Lottie and Suli went for a walk through the municipal park.

They sat on a bench by the fountain. He showed her the few photographs he had brought with him – his sisters, his schoolmates, his 25th birthday. He explained how he had managed to get to England on a holiday visa, with an invitation from someone who pretended to be his aunt.

'I wish I could treat you Lottie but I live on asylum seeker vouchers. And some cash I earn from washing up.'

'It's ok. But it's ... I've been going out with Mark for three years. We're supposed to be an item and you are complicating things.'

He walked over to the municipal flowerbeds and picked a daisy and brought it back to slip into the knot of her hair.

Another week found her in Suli's room, drinking tea with her feet up on his bed. They were two young people fascinated by each other. He pulled the torn curtains across the window and locked the door. She stretched out on the covers and watched him from the corners of her eyes.

For two weeks, Suli saved up the kebab wages. He looked

in the window of the pawnshop at the jewellery on display. Some of these are probably Sierra Leone diamonds he thought. Not that I could ever buy them. Inside, the suited woman with a silver chignon showed him earrings pinned to a blue velvet stand. There was one pair shaped like roses in silver with a pale pink stone in the centre. She said it was rose quartz, as she wrapped them up in grey tissue paper. He waited outside the bar. The sun was strong and he closed his eyes to let the heat wash over his face. A shadow cut the sun off. He opened his eyes and a tall young man with bristles of red hair stood over him.

'It's you isn't it?' He put his hands on his hips and stood bouncing on the front of his trainers. 'Listen. That's my bitch. You fuck off out of it.'

Suli watched him. Perhaps he had a knife in his pocket. You couldn't know. But he didn't look strong. I could take him he thought. He'd been in fights at school but that was years ago. The boy was taller than him but thinner.

He stood up. He shouldn't do this. The pastor had spoken against violence. Turn the other cheek. He tried to look unthreatening but it was quite possible that the boy thought, just because he was black, that he was aggressive.

'I don't know what you mean.'

'Yes you do – you fucker.'

Suli could smell the alcohol on his breath, so he had had to take a drink before doing this. Did Lottie know? She would be out in a minute.

'I don't want trouble,' Suli said. He walked away but angry with himself. If the police were called, he was afraid they'd beat him up and put him in a cell. He felt this red haired man watching him. He'll feel big now, Suli thought, like a big man.

When he got back to his room in the hostel, he opened up the tissue and let the earrings rest on the table. He felt so defeated he couldn't face the chatter in the kitchen, as people came and went with food and dirty plates. He lay down and took out his Bible. The Lord is my shepherd, though I walk in the valley of darkness... He hoped that somehow Charlotte would call for him. That he would hear her soft voice through the door – Suli honey, Suli honey.

*   *   *

'Hey man,' said Claude. From somewhere he had got a six-pack. He pulled the ring-pull off one and passed it over. They were eating rice drizzled with a little chili sauce. 'I might be able to help you.'

'How so?'

'In the bar where I collect the glasses, there is a woman who always looks at me. She is often on her own. I think she must be very lonely or turned out by her people or some such thing. Maybe she has a special thing for black men. She talks to me.'

'And why don't you want to try this marriage thing with her?'

'I've decided to go home. If I can get some cash out of the agency, maybe I could set up a business. Too cold here.

Too grey. You want to meet her?'

'What is she like?'

'She is somewhat older than us but she looks good.'

Suli sucked his teeth but nodded.

Claude got Suli into the club through the fire exit at the back. The woman was on the first floor, sipping a multi-coloured drink with a small umbrella in it. Suli introduced Claude and she passed him her drink. Claude could see her eyes already glittered with alcohol. He asked her to dance. She was slim and tall, but with lines on her face that made her look worried. Her perfume was very strong. It was like the scent of roses intensified a thousand times. She wore two gold chains around her neck. They lay on a spiky collarbone.

'I know what you want,' she said when she danced close to him. 'I'm divorced and I've got a teenage son but I'd like someone – you're very sweet.'

'I haven't got any money. I can't pay you.' He put his arm around her waist and they swiveled their hips together in a half turn.

'I want to piss my ex-husband off.' Suli laughed at her audacity.

'Would you really marry me?' He felt astounded at how lightly people did things here sometimes.

'It's no big deal. I get a handsome hunk to keep me warm at night and you get your papers.'

He wondered if she was saying these things because she

was drunk or angry at her husband. The tempo of the music changed and he danced around her, moving one foot forward then the next, undulating to the rhythm. He felt anxious about his mother and what she would think if she knew. She didn't have to know. He was a man. He had to make his own decisions. He could get to know her, perhaps like her before marrying. I could always change my mind, he thought.

Sheila had an old car and drove him to the hostel. She lit a cigarette for herself and opened the windows so the smoke rose into the warm night air.

'I appreciate your offer, really I do and I like you but I would like to get to know you more.' He wasn't sure if he could face this but if he liked her. Otherwise what was it? He thought about some of the people he'd met in the hostel – ones who'd walked across the Sahara, ones who'd crossed the sea in old fishing boats, the ones who hadn't made it but it didn't stop him thinking somehow that what he was doing stank.

'Are you a Christian?'

She laughed 'My grannie used to take me to church sometimes. I don't know if I am or if I'm not. Does it matter?'

'Yes, it matters to me.'

She exhaled and stayed silent.

'Don't think you're marrying some rich old bitch.' She said. 'I work in a Job Centre and you'll have to pull your weight.

You'll have to get on with my son. Earn some cash. Help at home. That kind of thing. I'm not the Queen of Sheba.'

He felt for the earrings in his pocket in their crinkly tissue paper. He wondered if she could hear the sigh of the paper. From the other side of town he heard the scream of a police siren and then he pulled the package out of his pocket and placed it on her lap.

'For the Queen of Sheba,' he said.

The Stone Dress

Maeve pushed the buggy through the fabric department. The bolts of cloth stood statuesque - magenta, emerald, orange, turquoise, sunshine yellow, purple, cerise, scarlet. She lifted one bolt of rayon silk in a fuchsia pink and held it against her face as she stood by the mirror. Her face was pale, mauve in the shadows against this unforgiving colour but the inside of her lips reflected back the bright rose of the fabric. She carried it to the counter and the assistant unwound it, spilling its silk with deft hands as she measured four yards against the brass ruler inlaid into the wooden surface. It made her think of a sky at dusk, flaming over the darkening stripes of the land.

'It's a lovely colour,' said the sales assistant.

'It's a colour I wear when I'm down.'

The bird like woman looked up over her specs. 'Is that so?' she murmured as she folded the yards into four and then eight squares that shimmered lipstick-brash under the fluorescent lights. Maeve slipped the package into the bottom trolley of the buggy and went to find matching cotton threads.

The reels were stacked in rows like tiny light bulbs, in which they shaded from one colour into another, from muted to sharp. She thought about the long journey the cotton twine had made from field to factory to department store and all the people employed in between.

She held a reel against the cloth she'd bought. They matched. The reel was sealed by paper circles at both ends and stamped with a logo of three oyster shells and Sylko, the English Sewing Co. 100 yards. Exactly 100 yards, like the fastest race in the world and she saw herself piercing the paper with the spike on the treadle and the whirr as she got the rhythm going, zipping down the seams of the rayon, her fingers feeding its silk to the metal teeth.

While Michael gurgled in his bouncer, Olive would have her face level with the arm and its up and down needle, her big, dark eyes wide with wonder as her mother transformed a lake of fuchsia into a sheath of silk, shaped by darts and hung with a slight cowl around the neck.

Olive would say 'This is my best colour Mummy.' Because it looked to her like Barbie pink, girly pink but Maeve would see how it imprisoned her, how it pinned her down, how a man's eyes would strip the pink off her, like skinning a mink of its fur.

Yes, she would use the same pattern. It was classy. The last one had got ripped. She'd make sure this one wasn't.

She loved jeans but when she was working, she felt her whole body was covered with a skin hard as rock, so she had to wear fabric to camouflage it. Jerome called it her stone dress, that it was something she zipped herself into when she left them. She put it on after she'd got the children ready for bed and read them their favourite story, tucking them in like sausages.

She pulled a raincoat over it as she threaded her way to the taxi rank that dropped her outside the Metropole. The bar glittered like granite in the mellow lights of the Tiffany glass. She curved on her stool like the women in the flowing robes of the brass Art Deco lamps. The reflection of her dress sparkled in the sides of her glass when a trick bought her a Manhattan or a Pimms or a Cuba Libra.

When she took off her dress for a client, she knew they couldn't see the rock face of her skin – sandstone in some lights, quartz in others. They imagined it was flesh they were touching and buried their jet-lagged, indulged faces in granite and rock. They were sliding down the cliff face of her.

Sometimes when a client lay heaving on top of her, his Chanel for Men choked her and she imagined she had turned into one of those stone figures she'd seen in pictures of the Rockies or even one of those huge Buddhas she'd seen on a TV programme about some far away country.

'Would you like another drink in my room?' he whispered to her as she slid off the stool and pulled down her dress. She saw the barman in the mirror polishing glasses and watching them. She followed Jaffer as he called himself up the carpeted steps at the end of the wide space of bar, past an enormous vase of lilies and broad green leaves. The scene stayed in her head as they waited for the lift. Inside he pulled up her dress and put his hands down her tights. She felt like pushing his silk suited body into the mirror at the rear of the lift so that it shattered into a spider's web of cut lines and fragments of glass, so that each would reflect sections of their cerise and dark grey bodies in tiny fragments, like the kaleidoscope she'd loved to play with when she was a little girl. She stroked his tie.

'My fee is £150.'

He remained silent until the lift stopped at the third floor and she followed him along the carpeted corridor, her heels silent in the thick pile of the carpet, till he opened the door to his room.

He poured her a whisky and went to shower, returning in a crisp, white dish dash that flowed over the curve of his belly.

'You can go shower now,' he said in his soft voice, slowly shaping the vowel sounds, stretching them out. It was an order she obeyed, locking the bathroom door while she washed, making the time last as long as possible. She hung the pink dress on the hook on the back of the door and went out to join him.

'Very nice. Very nice,' he whispered as she sat down on the bed and he pulled her over, pressing her down into the counterpane.

She was Triassic rock – immobile for millions of years. Whole ice-ages had come and gone while different tribes had invaded and left and all their blood and tears had been rained off her surface again and again.

It was only when she'd washed off the man sweat from her body and gathered the soft skins of her underwear from the floor, slipping into the stone dress and stood by the door that she remembered why she was there. Was he going to pay her? He eased himself from the bed, a melancholy smile across his face and he leaned for his wallet in the pocket of his jacket.

Sliding down the lift chute and through the mahogany lobby, with its emerald shades and purple shadows, she plaited her path through the crowds and the stone dress softened in the rain. She became skin and particle and muscle and nerves as she slipped her key into the door, walked through to lay her damp head against the sleeping heads of her children and breathe in their clean smell. Jerome rose from the TV to hold her in his arms and she leaned against the familiar shape of his body.

'Take off your dress baby, you're home now.' Then she unzipped her stone dress. The pile of fuchsia lay like a pool of blood on the carpet and she took the notes from her purse and hid them in a tin box she kept up the chimney breast.

But each week and month that she did what she did, she knew it was becoming harder and harder to take the dress off. She thought she might be turned to stone because she'd looked, looked with a cold, clear eye at the Medusa, when really it was safer to turn away to see reflections, to pretend it was nothing, it meant nothing and they needed it and she was just keeping them all together so they could live good. Those men they were chimeras, cartoons, characters in a B film. Blink your eye and they were gone. But Jerome, he was not gone and he seemed to think she could zip in and out of flesh and stone. She lay awake in the early hours, the yellow street light casting shadows in the room and thought how the stone dress held her, gripped her like some ancient method of restraint or torture, how what had seemed translucent was hardening into hard, unbreakable rock.

Back

This is not an apology but I want to know how you died.

I'm at the forty year reunion, with the sunshine of the south diffusing through white canvas, lighting up our ageing faces as we drink the palest of lime green Prosecco.

The hills beyond the campus are luscious, the hills we never walked on. You, Bobby, played your guitar to me under the pier, the waves slamming, percussive on the pebbles like a back beat. Or we were holed up in grubby digs, our mouths tasting of the chemical flavour of cheap instant coffee and cigarettes. The ashtrays were full of broken bits of cigarette, dissected to roll joints. Did we eat anything? But we never walked on these hills listening for nightingales.

We danced in the purple lights of some thrown together disco, our unwashed bodies close and sticky. Sometimes you played in the student bar, your dark curls falling over your face as you bent to the guitar, your Dagenham vowels curling round the empty words we felt so meaningful.

You showed me how to shoot up. I was scared even though the ritual was enticing. Despite the outward trappings of anarchic rebellion, there was a sensible, Northern girl inside, who looked to the future and what it might offer. You were sallow with infection. Philosophy hadn't taught you to ask the right questions.

Your friend Troy, your once friend, knocks against me but doesn't recognise me. He's still as skinny as he was when he came back from India in a coat of many colours. His eyes are just as narrow and calculating blue. His hair is grey now and tied into a ponytail.

Waiters in black waistcoats rotate through the marquee filling up glasses and their bubbles sparkle like surf on a summer day. We're the spoilt children of the sixties, who have never known war, never been out of work, never known hunger, not really. We thought we'd die before we got old. Only you have. I touch Troy on the arm and introduce myself but he doesn't remember me. We manage to gossip about lecturers and mutual friends. I bring your name up.

'Bobby Cook?' he pauses to sip his Prosecco. 'Yeah, he stayed in the area, in Sussex.'

'Is he here? Have you seen him?'

He actually gives me eye contact. 'Yeah, well he died.'

I can feel my heart rate quickening into a thudding rhythm. 'How? What happened?'

Troy was cool in red flares and a leather jacket and he came onto me in the student bar. He was quick, clever and witty. You, Bobby, were zonked out in your digs with the winter gale banging the flimsy windows against the frames. *Being and Nothingness* flapped open beside the bed, a needle on the chair.

Troy and I caught the bus into Brighton and walked along

Old Steine to a disco. He twirled my long brown hair in his fingers and we shook our bodies to the Stones. As we sang along to Let's Spend the Night Together he pulled me to him and we did, and the next night and the next. I'd left you, in the careless ways of those days. Troy actually wrote essays so we met in the library and compared notes. By the end of the month he was bored with me. The next time I saw him, he was crossing the campus with someone girlier. I never saw either you, Bobby or Troy again. I felt ashamed, I think, so stuck to my flat and flatmates and seminars.

Troy works for Brighton Council he tells me. I have to suppress my giggles. So this is what the fiery anarchist has ended up doing, sorting out parking problems and making sure potholes get filled in. He doesn't ask me what I do for a living.

'Bobby. Did he leave a family when he died?'

He's chewing crackling from the hog roast. I see he's not an ayurvedic vegetarian anymore.

'Yeah, he had a woman, a head teacher, I think.'

So he knows the situation. People who were students in the same year would know each other if they'd stayed in the area. But if you lived far away like me who'd moved north, you were out of the loop. I take a business card out of my handbag and press it to him.

'Please would you find out and let me know?'

He's seen someone more interesting to talk to and he's not

giving me eye contact anymore.

'OK must go now, just seen an old flat mate.' He swivels on his Timberlands and strides away, his black leather jacket shrinking to the corners of the marquee and I'm feeling dizzy. Sometimes it's dangerous to journey into the past.

I have a feeling that he knows how Bobby died. There was something on his face, like a passing shadow. He won't tell me, I'm sure. There was something about the way he talked of your 'woman' as if his mouth was full of chocolate éclairs.

The chatter around me hums like an orchestra tuning up, so I go outside with my glass and look around at the students, who are spread out on a knoll beneath the library, young and multi-national in light summer clothes, gossiping, flirting, discussing, plotting, their faces smooth and their hearts not turned to stone yet.

I walk along the prom and call my husband, the breeze echoing into the phone, distorting his voice, that comforting voice with its Yorkshire rhythms.

'Yeah, fine,' I say. Pause. 'A few old flatmates. Sumptuous.' I can hear Radio 4 on in the background. He'll be in the kitchen with a bottle of red wine on the go. The Northern Echo will be open on the worktop. as he checks the reporting of any criminal cases he knows of. The skies are clear, he tells me and he can see the shoulders of the Pennines.

I pull my hair away from my face and say. 'I'm going to stay another night. Ran into my old flat mate, Siobhan. You remember? Need to catch up on thirty something years.'

Back

'Oh come on Jan there's no point wallowing in the past.'

I'm approaching Burlington Square where Bobby and I used to spend time in my room in the big shared flat. The previous squalor would be unimaginable to the current inhabitants, in their shockingly white houses with slatted, wooden shutters and tree ferns on the balconies. I end the conversation with the husband; there are many things I never talk about with him, as he doesn't like difficult, intimate revelations.

In what used to be an ice-cream parlour, I spoon the froth off a cappuccino and look out at the sea lit with flames of sunset. I feel hollow, like a burst balloon and for why? Bobby, I whisper, I haven't seen you for nearly thirty seven years. How was your life? Did you get clean and try to be happy? What happened to your music?

He was a self contained man. The music, his heroin, his watchful cynicism, they cut him off from people but we talked, we connected, as they say and I was moved by his vulnerability. Why am I still here, pulled like a fish caught on a hook to I know not what end?

In the morning I walk into the town centre, enjoying the salt smell in the air, the echoes of rock and roll from the fat pier and then turn into the Lanes for another nostalgic ramble, when I see Troy coming out of an antique shop with a woman. They're laughing and he touches her arm to guide her into the next turning. She's short with a blonde bob and a black trouser suit, high wedge heels, the trousers flapping about her calves as she keeps up with him.

'Hi!' I shout hurrying, shivering a little as the buildings cut out the sun on my bare arms, 'Troy!' The blonde has turned now and is looking towards me, while Troy has that puzzled frown on his face again. Then I realise I have no idea why I'm calling him or what I'm going to say to him. I catch up and reach out to touch him, God knows why, but he flinches and leans back.

'Sorry to bother you,' I say. 'Don't forget I really want to know how Bobby died, it's important to me.' I notice the blonde staring, looking from Troy to me and back again. He mumbles something like Ok Ok into the collar of his dark pink shirt and turns to go, pulling on her hand. I stare at their retreating backs, gradually losing sight of them in the holiday melee of day trippers. I see her turn back briefly to look at me.

The Lanes lead me on and I wander past where the chaplaincy used to be. Sometimes I went to Mass there and made a good friend, Siobhan. I don't practise any more of course, I'm a sort of Buddhist now. Well I find the notion of not wanting much very helpful. Not desiring. Just being where you are. Siobhan wasn't at the reunion but I remember she came back to Brighton and that the address was in Kemptown, so I turn east, trying to catch the ghost of myself, young, pretty, fashionably nihilistic, silly with petty worries, striding down the street with long hair blowing in the wind off the Channel, arm in arm with a tall, dark haired, brown-eyed man with a guitar over his shoulder and a slight stoop, who rubs his upper teeth against his bottom lip, anxiously.

I remember Siobhan's address and knock on the red painted door of her beautiful Georgian house. A window in the second floor slides up and a head of curly, grey hair leans out. 'Yes?' it says. I wave and tell her who I am. We stare at each other, trying to locate the real faces through the masks of skin we're wearing, masks with lines and grooves.

'Bloody Hell Jan. It's only because it's half term that you found me in.'

We drink fennel tea on the balcony and she shows me photos of her daughter who is on a gap year, her son who's a doctor in London and photos of her second wedding, ten years ago. We gossip about people we both knew when we were students, until I bring up the subject of Bobby.

'You remember, I went out with him in my final year – tall, played the guitar, thick black hair, cockney accent, unusually working class for this place.'

'Yes, him. I forgot you went out with him. It wasn't long was it? Didn't you go out with Troy? He's still around Brighton, very much so. Not that we socialise. I'm too involved with the Church, all that Justice and Peace stuff. Liberal lefties like him are very intolerant.'

'He knows what happened to Bobby. I'm sure he does. Bobby died.'

'How?'

'He said he'd find out and let me know.'

'Why do you need to know?' she looks at me over the top of her glasses.

'I'm not sure. I just do.' I pull my chair into the shade as the midday sun is intense.

'It rings a bell. Something in the paper. There was a link to Sea Life, because he worked there.'

'Sea Life? Yes, I could see he'd be happier surrounded by silent moving creatures. Could we look on line Siobhan? Please.' She looks at me oddly, like I'm unstable or something but she brings me into what she calls the office, climbing over mounds of paper files. I try The Argus archive as Siobhan thinks he had a name as a local musician. I don't know how long I spend sliding through screens of past main stories. I can hear Siobhan stacking things in the kitchen.

'No,' the word comes out more of a sob than language. 'He killed himself. He was found hanged there.'

'Look,' says Siobhan, pointing at the screen. 'There's a photograph of his wife, making a statement about him, how talented he was.'

I look at the image. It's the woman I saw with Troy.

'I know her slightly, she's a head teacher. I didn't know she was married to Bobby,' Siobhan says.

'Yes. I know.' She looks at me. 'I saw her this morning, arm in arm with Troy.'

We fall silent. Chatter from balconies and gardens along the street float past us. I can't speak, just sip on my mug of tea and fight back tears. Siobhan looks kindly at me.

'I have to go, sorry. I'll be in touch.' She lets me out into the sunshine and I walk down the street to the sea front. The sense of loss and emptiness and regret and, yes, love, swirl around inside as if they were real liquids sloshing up against each other. It's so physical I have to lean against a railing in case I fall over. The tide is going out and it will be coming back in tomorrow when I leave and it will be going out again by the time I get home.

Landscape

Lennie was in a duffel coat outside the cinema. She noticed that his dark hair had been brylcreamed and shone like a Roman helmet. He stubbed out his cigarette with his shoe and pulled her inside to the ticket desk.

The usherette shone her torch and led them to the back. She could smell the sweat in his clothes as he leaned to pass pop-corn. There was a whirr from the projecting box above them. When Josie looked up at the dust motes in its glare she felt Lennie's arm go round her shoulders. He'd danced with her at an inter-grammar school dance last year before he went to work on the buses, some smoochy number and he'd pushed his mouth against hers, before any teacher could see and call out his real name of Leonardo. She remembered his teeth in her lip. She stared at Marilyn Monroe's huge, heart-shaped face but he pulled her head back and forced his mouth onto hers. She felt his teeth and tongue inside her mouth. She wriggled her tongue into his to see what would happen. He moved to her neck and sucked into the flesh. His hand then moved over her blouse and skirt. Each time she pushed off his hand, it returned like a snake.

'I want to see the film, this bit with Jack Lemmon's funny. Leonardo.' She hissed the syllables and noticed a smirk on his face, as he slipped his hand under her skirt to the stocking tops.

Afterwards he stood with her at the bus stop and held her in a vice like grip.

'Give over,' she said. 'I want a tab,' and took one of his Capstans.

'That were nice, Josie. Shall I see you next Saturday? Might treat you again. Schoolgirl n all.'

She looked up at his pretty face, the soft lips and dark eyes that mirrored the street light.

'Got nowt else to do.'

He raised his eyebrows and blew smoke at her.

'Get up Josie. It's time for school.' Her mother banged on the door. Condensation trickled down the windows. Josie spun into a thick dressing-gown but she still shivered.

'Bugger, there's no hot water,' she said to the mirror as she rubbed it with the sleeve of her dressing-gown. The bathroom smelt of shit and mint toothpaste. She could feel a spot coming on the back of her neck so she dabbed it with spittle on toilet paper and then spiked up the Jean Seberg haircut with her fingers.

The school navy skirt got expertly rolled over the waist and she left the top button of her shirt undone. She squashed her school hat into the bag.

'You look scruffy Josie. Why isn't your shirt done up?'

Josie ignored this, chucking it into what she called her rubbish bin of bourgeois stuff. 'Dad gone?'

'He took the lorry. When's the exam?'

'May. Why?'

'Yer Dad wants to know. He's going to ask at the firm if there's an opening for you. In the office like?'

'Office? I'm not going to a bloody office.'

Her mother was holding the iron and it swung.

'Less of the swearing. Is that what they teach you in sixth form?'

'Dad swears all the time.'

'He's the breadwinner and he's a man.'

Her mother stared, eyes cold as envy. Josie stared back unflinching. She watched her mother tie on a pinny and go out into the freezing scullery to iron.

Her brother Brian loomed into the kitchen. At sixteen he was taller than her, with the same auburn hair shaved short at the back. He spread a piece of cold toast with margarine and jam.

'Why were you strapped last week?' Josie sipped her tea.

'How'd you know about that?'

'I do have friends with brothers at your school.'

'Weren't nowt. Them as asks no questions don't get..' and he flicked her on the head with his toast. 'Saw you going into the pictures with lecherous Iti Lennie.'

'What's it to you? And what's all this Iti rubbish?'

'Don't want word round you're a tart. Miss high and mighty.'

Josie noticed how much he looked like Dad with his thick neck and dark eyebrows that met in the middle like a murderer's. Sometimes she felt she saw a look of dislike across her Dad's face and sometimes when he looked her up and down it made her skin crawl.

She slid into school assembly just in time. Her mind drifted in an out of the Headmistress's talk. University for those who could pass exams would open up a world of opportunity. She never mentioned the life of an artist but at least she didn't bang on about marriage like her mother or aunties.... When yer get married then yer'll know what's what.....

She sucked the end of her tie and looked across at Wendy. As they marched out of the hall, she squeezed next to her.

'Lennie took me to the pictures,' whispered Josie.

'Not smarmy Lenny on the buses?'

'He looks like Elvis. And yes, his family's Italian, like da Vinci you know, you div.'

'He's went out with all the thick girls in the fifth form!'

Mrs. Gross rushed into class, her worn academic gown blowing with the movement. Her dark hair was rolled up into a chignon and she played with a string of pearls as she talked through the Waste Land's scene, in which the secretary has casual sex, without using the word sex.

Landscape

'Would the poet be less critical if the woman was an artist Miss?'

Josie questioned this teacher, whose words she loved, whose thoughts about literature and its characters and images, filled her life with hope.

'You think he despises the banality of these people's lives?'

'Something like that Miss. Like maybe it's OK for posh people to break rules.'

'Perhaps he's just presenting it as an example of how life has become corroded and meaningless.'

It didn't have to be like that. She'd been in the top three in the class all the way up school. She looked at her teacher's handsome but worn face. She knew the rumour that Mrs. Gross had made a bad marriage and was now a divorcee with a grown-up son.

During dinner break, Josie went to the art room and worked on the clay figure of Anthony from her A level play. She used a spatula to shape grooves on the angular features. Mrs. Gross came in holding a mug of tea.

'I heard about this head. It's good Josie.'

'Enough to get me into college?'

'Have you told your parents? You know I think you should go to university.'

'I know but... I want to be creative. If I go to university I'll end up a teacher.'

Mrs. Gross lifted her head of pinned-up hair and smiled but only one side of her mouth lifted.

After school Wendy and Josie waited for the bus together in the thickening fog. They pulled their thin coats tight and put their reddening hands into the pockets.

'So? What was lover boy like? Did yer have to fight him off?'

'You can talk. You and Bernie.'

'Bernie loves us.'

'Bernie's trying to stop you getting to university.'

'Well p'raps it's not for the likes of us. I could train as a secretary. We could save up to get married.'

'Bloody hell Wendy. You're only eighteen. The whole world's out there.'

She heard her mother's voice from the kitchen. 'Have you finished the brass?' Josie pushed the grimy rags and Brasso into the cloth bag. Her mother's wedding presents gleamed.

I've got to tell them I'm going to go to Art College she thought. He can roll that in his cigarettes. But they can't stop me.

She banged down the bag of cleaning stuff on the kitchen table next to where her mother was peeling potatoes. The radio was full of laughter but the flesh on her mother's face hung down in grooves. She took a deep breath, listening to the plop of a skinned potato as it fell into the bowl of water.

'Mum. I've decided. I'm going to Art College after A levels. Not teacher training.'

'Are you off your rocker? Whatever for?' Her mother's red lipstick had left a stripe on the end of the cigarette that lay on the Blackpool ashtray.

'It's what I want to do. It's what I'm good at.'

'Your Dad might have something to say. We can't pay for you to be swanning about with a bag of paints. In my day you did what your parents told you.' She carried on peeling the potatoes with increased speed and slammed the potatoes into the water. Josie spun round, grabbed her coat off the rack and ran out the door. She headed to the town theatre where she was helping to paint the scenery.

This was another world away from school and home. The inside of the room in the Osborne play had already been drawn in. All she had to do was apply the colours. She pulled her overalls around her and quickly got absorbed in the process, each brushstroke painting out the tension and panic she felt.

'Josie, my love, that's gorgeous.' She looked up to see Jimmy, the male lead, wearing a silky cravat tucked into the neck of his cream shirt. 'There's no need to kneel. I may be the principal actor but..'

Josie giggled but the tear, that had been inside her eye since the row with her mother, slipped out. He wiped her cheek. 'Pretty girl like you shouldn't have tears, in the prime of your life.'

She concentrated on the gingham squares. This sense of dislocation with her family was frightening and inexplicable. Had she been left with them by gypsies?

'You don't know what I'm going through.'

'Well you could tell Jimmy about it. Let me to buy you lunch in the Dog and Parrot.'

He was waiting outside in his sports car. The roof was down and she slid into the leather seats. The wind whipped her face as they tore down the high street. Every bugger's looking at me she thought, as they swung into the pub car park.

'What would you like? Babycham? Martini?' As she'd never had a drink in a pub and didn't want to look stupid, she remembered Kim Novak ordering a whisky in a film.

'Whisky.'

Jimmy's eyebrows rose. 'Only eighteen and on the hard stuff. What other surprises do you have in store my lovely? I've ordered scampi in a basket. Ok?'

Josie smiled at him. She'd never eaten them before. She forced herself to swallow down the whisky between mouthfuls of scampi, though it made her dizzy and sweaty.

'We could go for a spin.' If I were doing his head, she thought, I'd have to get that Roman nose just right and the lines at the side. I wonder how old he is. Not as old as my Dad but much older than me.

Landscape

They passed the factories beyond the estate where she lived, the smoke curling up into the clouds and then they twisted along the narrow roads, roaring round corners and up over blind bridges till they reached the first peak. He pulled into a layby. She looked down on the city and its people milling about like Lowry figures and she laughed into the wind. Jimmy took her hand.

'I'd like a taste of that whisky you've just thrown down.' He pulled her towards him and kissed her. Josie compared kisses. This was like velvet she thought, you sink into it. Lennie's was like a nylon mac.

'There's something about you Josie. You've got a spark. But careful you don't set yourself on fire.' He stroked her coarse, spiky hair and she breathed in shirt fabric and heard the beat of his heart like a snare-drum.

'I'm still at school. No chance of me catching fire there. But I'm going places.' What is it, she thought, am I a jam jar that these men are buzzing around me? I don't even wear make-up and my fingers are always dirty with clay or paint. But so what? He might be older than me but the world might end in a huge nuclear blast next week.

'Would you take me to a jazz club? I've never been.'

'Jazz. It's not really my thing but if that's what you want, why not?'

She looked down into the valley, where the lights were beginning to come on, and then switched into close focus, to his hands, which had, she noticed, rather plump fingers that were undoing the buttons on her blouse.

Sword Beach

I didn't want to throw up in the tent so I got out of the sleeping bag and hauled myself through all the debris on the floor. My head vibrated with orange light as the sun streamed through the cotton ceiling. I vomited into the blackberry bushes. The smell of coffee hit me. People were already up, chattering, and a bloody blackbird was giving it in a tree nearby.

Had I really eaten so much? It was the Calvados passed round the campfire when the beer ran out. I hoped my kids wouldn't wake up. I vomited again and sensed disapproving eyes over today's Le Figaro. I was everything they already thought about English women.

Yes, it had been Ben's idea to go camping, to take the Granddad he hardly knew to the war beaches. He hadn't met my father until he was twelve, so they were strangers and I was trying, Dad was trying, to get a relationship into gear. I wished I hadn't lost my rag with him when we were putting up the Meccano poles for the sodding tent. I never liked camping, but at least it was a cheap holiday. If he'd had a proper father, he'd have been doing it. Instead my Dad and Ben had to work out the mechanics between them. My mouth felt disgusting even after rinsing out with a swig of water.

Zoe was the first to wake up. Ben would emerge from

hibernation later. He was a teenager, just, after all. Once I heard Zoe stirring, I got into action and lit the gas to get water on the boil. I suddenly remembered my Dad. He'd had a drink or two last night – what had happened to him? He seemed to disappear at one point.

'Mum, you smell horrible. What is it?' She still had that little girl sweetness

'Just a bit sick, something I ate, probably.'

'I had a nice time playing out with Therese and we made a dam in the stream, even though we can't say much. My feet got really cold.'

I rubbed her feet between my hands. The nails were still like small shells that I sometimes let her put varnish on. The two of them had been in the stream till far too late, but with the drink and music, I'd forgotten she was out in the dark. What was I doing? She held a bowl while I poured water into it and I chucked it over the bushes.

I thought if I could just get the breakfast ready then I could take my sleeping bag outside and lie down in the shadow of the tent. Then I heard my Dad whistling, as he cut through the campsite, with a baguette under his arm and a plastic of milk. He was wearing those strange shoes, halfway between trainers and moccasins with squashy soles, so his feet didn't hurt.

'All right Denise?' He grinned from ear to ear. 'Bye, you look rough.'

I poured boiling water on the tea bags. 'Not too chilly for you at night Dad?'

'Brought my thermals. What's that smell?'

I said nothing while I assembled frying pan and bacon.

'Nothing a cup of tea won't solve, love.' He pulled apart a folding chair and eased his sizeable bulk onto the striped canvas. 'You can certainly put it away.'

'I didn't lick it off the ground, did I?' I passed him a bacon sandwich.

Between mouthfuls, he pulled a small map out of his jacket pocket. 'I've checked the map – one road from here to Falaise.'

I knew Ben was excited about going to the old battle grounds with his granddad, though he found it hard to imagine this overweight, balding man with arthritic hands, in the uniform of the East Yorkshire Regiment, fighting for his life in Normandy. War films and history lessons – somehow they didn't translate into the old man he was getting to know, with his Match of the Day and a pint of Boddingtons. We'd already visited Caen where, he told us, the battle was even fiercer than on Sword beach and he'd lost more of his friends in the Division. He also wanted to see Falaise, where there'd been another bloody battle in which his best friend, Reggie, had been killed.

When we got to Falaise, the market was in full swing. The stalls glittered with jars and bowls holding the crown jewels –

olives like jade and jet beads, raspberries like tiaras of rubies and artichokes, stacked like a bowl of agate. The air was thick with the smell of burning butter as the crepe stalls got it going.

'We fought the Germans through this square – Look, that's were the snipers were, in the Church bell tower.' He fingered the rough bullet holes in the church walls, gouged out chunks of brick and mortar. Ben felt inside the holes too.

'Awesome,' said Ben. 'Where did all the blood go?'

'My mate Reggie got killed over there. A grenade.' He pointed to La Mairie, now white like a wedding cake decorated with tricolour flags. I looked at him closely. In my childhood he'd never talked about these things and now, I suppose, with age and distance, he wanted to remember, to pass on that experience to us, to the future. I couldn't see his eyes but then I couldn't remember, growing up, ever really looking into his pale, grey eyes. You just didn't have that kind of intimacy with a Dad. But the moment passed as the kids soon got excited about eating French chocolates.

On the way home the Normandy fields and farms glowed lush and dark green in the dusk. Cows, the colour of clotted cream, chewed, plump and peaceful. Apples ripened in the orchards like spawn in their jelly waiting to come alive.

After we'd eaten our potatoes and tinned stew, the kids were sent to the block to wash up.

'Go easy on the sauce tonight, love,' he said. I rolled my

eyes, muttering under my breath. It's not easy to have your failings pointed out.

'But anyway, you're...' He started to say something intimate, but couldn't deal with it.

'What? Anyway where did you skedaddle off to last night?'

He tapped his finger at the side of his nose like an extra in a war film set in Italy.

Day five was our trip to the beaches, in particular Sword Beach. Dad had pinned his D Day medals to his British Home Stores suit jacket. Ben was beside himself with vicarious excitement but I could see that Dad was trying to tell a truth, that he didn't want to glamorize it. We walked along the promenade, looking at the bright holiday homes and the fields beyond where a tractor was pulling a fishing boat up a track. The beach was dotted with umbrellas and parties of families, football games and children jumping the waves. Dad pointed out the remains of German gun emplacements and bunkers. We stopped at a memorial.

'So you had to get out of those landing craft and fight your way up?' asked Ben, looking far out to sea, where oil tankers ploughed the grey water.

'Yes after a night crossing, men being sick over the side, and the water was freezing and bloody. The beach was littered with tanks, burning vehicles, barbed wire, wounded men and the noise was deafening; bombs aimed at the German defences were exploding and from the Germans, gun fire and anti-tank mortar. I was shaking all over.'

'You never talked to us about this when we were kids Dad. And then you turned your back on me.' I didn't want to say more because I could feel Ben and Zoe listening.

'I'm pleased you came to look for me. Things got complicated and it was really your mother who was determined. As for the war, in a way I've tried not to think about it. But now, well, I'm getting on and I'd like young Ben and Zoe to know, to remember.'

Dad pointed beyond the dunes, where the marram grass rustled. A family had spread a blanket out with a table-cloth on top. Bowls were laid out and a red-faced man of my age was pouring glasses of wine. A screaming toddler ran towards the sea, chased by a pretty woman with long, fair hair. Dad waved to an elderly woman in a navy, spotted dress sat on one of the beach chairs. She was slicing bread with the loaf tucked under one arm. Her white hair, pulled into a symmetrical chignon, accentuated the tanned face and deep-set eyes, black as olives. Dad raised his straw trilby in greeting.

'Hello Mathilde,' he said.

'Bonjour Monsieur Joe. Ca va?' She pointed at his medals and smiled. Dad's face was like a firework that's just had its blue taper lit. I raised an eyebrow when I looked at him and he had the grace to look embarrassed. 'You don't remember this family? They were round the fire last night too. Mathilde and I got talking. She was thirteen when the British soldiers arrived in Falaise.'

'You're full of surprises Dad.' I linked arms with him.

There were concrete gun turrets sunk into the sand at the top of the dunes, askew and drunk, one eye leering. Ben bent to the dark gape.

'D'you think there are German bones in there Granddad?'

He stood still, saying nothing but, from the angle where I was stood, I could see one tear slip out the left corner of his pale eye and slide down a cheekbone into his jowl. I pressed his arm into me. There was nothing to say. He'd once told me he was one of only twelve of his platoon to survive. It was impossible for me to imagine how that felt or to be in a situation where it is kill or be killed. Kind of guilty I'd guessed and now, trying to imagine that moment, I thought about what he had done with the rest of his life. Had he earned the gift of life? Had he paid his dues? He'd been a kind of distant father but, perhaps that's how it was then. He and Mum had turned me out because of my other half. But he was trying now, before it was too late, I guess.

Zoe was getting restless with all this old people's stuff, so we lay down together and made a sausage, rolling down the side of the dune, grains of sand in our ears and hair and inside our jeans. Maybe these grains held someone's DNA, miniscule fragments of bone or blood.

The campfire socialising had begun by the time we got back to the camp site. Flames lit up the Gallic faces. Mathilde was with some of her family round the fire. She was poking at the logs, pushing some closer to the flames. She raised a glass in greeting when she saw Dad. The man who'd said he was a policeman in Paris, gave me a lop-sided smile and looked me up and down. I breathed in and straightened my still wiry posture.

Under the canopy of our tent, we managed to throw together some sausages and beans, hoping our neighbours couldn't see. Ben went off to play ping pong with the other kids on the site and Zoe trailed behind him, complaining. I asked Dad if he'd like to take his drink and sit by the fire with me.

'Don't overdo it love,' he said.

'I've a lot on my plate. Anyway, perhaps it's inherited.'

He looked away, couldn't meet my eyes and said nothing.

I felt ashamed.

'I know you went through the war Dad, I've been through a bloody war myself.'

'You've not told me much, just that… fellah.'

'Jimmy.'

'Yes him. He's away, isn't he?'

He didn't know the half of it but I didn't want to upset him, just said 'I'm glad that bastard's in prison. The things he did to me.'

It was hard for him I know. He'd rather not talk about

anything disturbing. Football, the weather, the roses, they were safe. Mostly. And there were all those years he'd skimmed over. If he'd been a different kind of man, perhaps, he would have hugged me at that point but he said 'Well, you're here, living and breathing. And it's good I've a chance to get to know the grandkids. Don't know if I deserve it.'

I nodded and looked to the fire, where that good-looking policeman was pouring a round of drinks.

'You're worth... you're worth more.' Dad struggled to find words for the kind of thing he'd never say. No, I thought, perhaps I won't get paralytic tonight and wake up with a gendarme out of his uniform.

Jerome

It had started at a wedding, a dance with a stranger. He didn't mean to damage anyone's life. These modern women, well, they got no loyalty.

He had rushed headlong on the journey to here, dramatically, hastily, voraciously, with a delight, with awe at the speed of things. Now he was surprised at the speed with which his body had disintegrated, since the first diagnosis.

Examination of conscience was not his style. Insouciance and courage in the face of death - though he had never called it courage and neither had anyone else. It was what you did in the world he lived in.

Through the window near his bed, trees curved and bent in the wind, scattering blossom of a kind he couldn't name. He'd never learned the names of English trees. Clouds and blue sky kaleidoscoped beyond. That at least he could name. As a child, after fierce games with his brothers, he'd swum on his back in the warm sea just watching the sky's dance.

The man next to him was still out from his operation. He was older, lined and grey looking. Tubes went into his wrists like he was wired to the wall.

'What kind of operation that?' he'd asked earlier.

'They're going to cut out some of my intestines,' the man had said. 'Cut out the cancer and attach a bag for the waste.'

What kind of living is that, he'd thought, what woman would want you with a bag of shit hanging from your belly? He pressed the click on the morphine; it made him feel less anxious. And then switched on the TV thinking it would be right for the York races at 3.30. Shame the nurses wouldn't put a fiver for him, both ways, on the Queen of Sheba. Now that was a hot tip from Marcus. He settled down to watch the jockeys and horses parade in the enclosure. The camera focused on a tick tack man shouting his odds. The Queen of Sheba was a glossy black thoroughbred, sixteen hands high with two white socks, ridden by an Irish jockey in purple and gold. He was mesmerised by the colour and excitement, the frantic commentary once the horses shot off.

'Damn. I never rode a horse. A donkey yes but a horse, no. I'd a liked that.'

He didn't see the two young people walking up the ward, two beautiful young people with smooth, flawless, brown skin, the girl with her hair braided, the beads in the end clacking as she walked. The young man's head was shaved to a number one and shone in the overhead lights of the ward.

'Dad,' they said together. He looked at them through the morphine and the commentary, where The Queen of Sheba was storming up on the inside, being chased by River of Light to the left. The breeze from the slightly open window blew curtains to a sigh. He tasted the dehydration of his tongue, the tense bitter ache for a cigarette, felt the cool cotton of the sheet folded over his belly, where the buttons of the pyjama top had become undone. It had to be Olive and Michael.

He sighed with exhaustion, 'Olive. Michael. How you find me?'

'Michael tracked down Curtis and he told us. We wanted to see you.'

Jerome gestured to the plastic chair for his daughter to sit down. Michael stood at the end of the bed. 'How are you?' he faced his father.

'Oh, you know. Ting and ting, I not ready to go.' His simple words silenced them.

'You haven't been looking after yourself,' said Olive, twirling some braids in her left hand. Her eyes were almond shaped like her mother's and she had the same heart shaped face and thick curving eyebrows. 'Surely there are more possible treatments, radiotherapy?'

'I try everything but it seems they don't work. It spread everywhere.'

'But is this where you should be, Dad?' Michael frowned, struggling to get the word out. He hadn't used that word for eighteen years. 'Perhaps a hospice somewhere?'

Jerome looked at them, taking in their health, their youth, their nice clothes.

'How's your mother?'

Olive smiled. 'She's fine Dad. She's happy, living in the countryside, selling her artwork.'

Jerome fell silent. Everyone could hear the noises of the ward, the televisions of two other patients, the chatter coming from the nurses' station outside in the corridor, a man whispering to his wife. There was no time to beat around the bush.

'She able to forgive me?' he turned to his two children, unsure what they knew, what they would admit to. But there was no time for fancy talk. 'Ask her for me. That all I want. And to see you two beautiful people. She did well.'

The Frock

The back yard was full of feathers. While Dad was plucking a turkey he got cheap from the market, she watched him in her Queen's Coronation T shirt and the green skirt made by her Mum badly from recycled corduroy. One thick red plait hung down her sturdy seven year old back. His hands rhythmically sent rows of orange, brown, yellow and tawny feathers flying in the damp air making it look like a byre, where animals might be kept, patiently waiting for something to happen. She wanted to ask him whether Father Christmas would bring her the pink frilly dress she wanted so much, but hunched over the plump, half-naked bulk of a turkey, she couldn't catch his eye.

The smell of sausages, bacon, black pudding and fried bread flew out from the kitchen back door, into the yard. It cut through the smog in the London air. The little girl folded her arms over the blue queen in a diamond crown, and a coronation coach and horses. It had been bought by her Uncle and Aunt who didn't shout at each other but spoke politely in soft voices. Would you like a cup of tea Patrick? Are you comfortable Maureen? I'm going up to bed, are you coming with me?

Her breath turned to smoke in the cold air and she stamped her feet, watching the turkey's head lying sideways on the slab, the pink bits lame, damp, somehow disgusting, and its claws like Great Auntie Nellie's fingers when she went to visit her in hospital.

'Jesus, Mary and Joseph, we'll having nothing to eat on Christmas Day. In God's name why did you buy a cheap turkey? From a market! Don't you know they're all crooks? Or was he a drinking crony?' He mother's voice bounced off the back yard wall.

'Jesus, I'm just trying to make Christmas nice. You, you appreciate nothing, you stupid woman. I should've married your sister. '

'Get in here Patty,' shouted 'You'll catch your death of cold, outside without a coat.'

Over her eggs and bacon the little girl tried to catch her mother's time but, in between the shouting from yard to kitchen and back and the older children coming in through the twisted crepe paper, hanging in the dingy hall, she had to seize a moment's pause.

'Mum, will Father Christmas bring the pink dress with the frills and bow?'

'Want doesn't get,' said her mother, basting another egg as the eldest girl slumped into the kitchen.

'No runny yolk,' said Eileen.

'No runny yolk, indeed. You should be glad of the food on your plate and eat it up. Have you polished the brass upstairs?'

'Yes Mum.'

'Well I'll try and get your hair in rags for ringlets before Midnight mass, if I have time.'

Dad brought the pockmarked turkey into the kitchen. There were still a few small feathers around the ankle.

'That thing stinks,' her mother spoke with her back to him, turning the sausages.

He rolled his eyes at Patty.

'It'll be great when it's cooked with gravy and stuffing, sausage meat and roast potatoes. Stop complaining woman and get on with it.'

'You'll be complaining when we sit down to eat our Christmas dinner without any meat. What did you swap to get this stinking turkey? A hot tip at the bookies? Some whiskey off the back of a lorry?'

He rubbed his moustache, yellowed by nicotine and then speared a piece of bacon with a fork onto the breadboard, peeled off two slices of white bread from their grease proof wrapper and rolled the bacon into a sandwich.

The dress was strawberry ice-cream pink with two layers of frills around the hem, a peter pan collar and puffed sleeves. The waist had two ribbon streamers that tied in a bow at the back. You'd expect a fairy to wear it floating on a cloud with a smile and a wand. She'd be able to swirl in it because the skirt would spin like a cloud of blossom. It would be the most beautiful dress in the street. It would shimmer in the wardrobe waiting to be worn, danced, and sung. The desire for the dress was eating her alive, like a fever. She didn't notice the smell in the kitchen, but bit into crisp, bacon fat, a dreamy look on her face.

'What's up my fairy elephant? You look as if you're seeing an apparition?'

'Dad, it's the pink dress I told you about. Do you think Father Christmas will get it for me?'

'Life's full of surprises, Patty, maybe he will, maybe he won't.' With that he was gone, like an apparition, his disembodied voice echoing back into the kitchen. 'I said I'd meet Brendan for a pint, I'll be back in time for Mass.'

'Maybe he'll be back for Midnight Mass, maybe he won't,' said her mother, clattering up the plates into the deep white sink.

Eileen leaned her scrawny arms into the sink to scour the dishes with a rag, while Patty wiped them and lay them on the table, an array of patterns, ladies in grey crinolines with pink bonnets, blue lovers escaping over Chinese bridges and chipped plates with blue and white stripes around the rim.

'Have you ever had a frilly dress Eileen?'

'Frilly? I had a lovely long dress and veil for my first holy communion and I've got cousin Moira's velvet dress for best. It has a white lace collar but you can't run in either of them, so boring.'

'But isn't it exciting to have such a dress Eileen?'

'Are you mad or what? You'd get it torn in no time at all

and then you'd be for it and where would you wear it? Are you intending to call in on the new Queen?' She flicked Patty on top of the head with the wet rag.

The four older children set out a game of rummy, half watching the variety show on television, their sides or backs glowing with the heat of the fire. In its flickering flames Patty saw a pink dress shimmering. The Toppers were kicking their legs and swirling round in their sparkly outfits as part of the show.

'I'd be able to dance like that if I had a swirly dress. I'd be like the girl with the red shoes. They'd have to cut the dress off me to stop me dancing.'

Michael, the baby, slept on his mother's knees as she watched the show, drawing on a cigarette with unusual concentration and stillness. A lock of dyed black hair fell over her forehead, where deep lines were etched.

'Well it's a terrible night to be walking to Midnight Mass if your father doesn't make it home from the pub. What time does the priest want you at church to get ready for serving, Jimmy?'

'11 o'clock mum'

'We should all walk down together and we could say the rosary till the Mass begins. When the show finishes all of you get upstairs and wash your hands and faces, and for God's sake Eileen brush that hair of yours, it looks like a bird's nest and then do Patty's plait.'

They waited in the hall while their mother buttoned up her wool coat and put on red lipstick, unsmiling, in the geometric shape of the hall mirror, a slight smudge on the skin around the narrow upper lip.

'What a useless husband,' she shouted into the dark house as she locked the door. It was bitterly cold and their breath came out as smoke in the filthy smog of the night.

'I've got black in my nose.' said Patty, shivering, as she pulled tight the raincoat tightly around her.

'Don't pull it too tight,' said her mother. 'You'll look like a sack of potatoes tied in the middle. Too much jam sponge!'

She and Eileen jumped over any cracked paving stones as they made their way, for you could never tell what bad luck they might bring you in the future.

'What if Father Christmas comes while we're at Mass?' asked Patty.

'He won't he has to get to Mass himself' said Jimmy.

What church does he go to?'

'Rome, sure, the Pope himself will give him communion.'

'Is it far from Rome to here? Will he have time to bring the presents?'

Patty thought about the novenas her mother often did, praying to turn your father into a sensible man, she would say. Perhaps she should have said a novena too, for the pink dress. Had she prayed hard enough? She'd been with her mother to many early morning masses. Wouldn't that be enough? But it didn't seem to make their father do the things he was supposed to do.

Their voices echoed along the streets of terraced houses and onto the main street where the traffic lights glimmered like fireflies. Buses roared out of the smog, a blur of lights and smoke.

'You see, I told you I'd get to mass.' Her father loomed out of the dark and swirled Patty round, dropping her down suddenly onto her sturdy feet. He reached out to put an arm round his wife.

'God, you smell of drink. What will Father Murphy say?'

'Oh woman, give it a rest, it's Christmas Eve and I've managed to get a few of the other things you wanted.'

Patty noticed he was carrying a large canvas bag on his back.

'Are you serving tonight Jimmy?' he asked.

'I always do'

'Well don't be smirking to the other altar boys tonight. Let's be proud to have a boy on the altar on Christmas Eve.'

Jimmy said nothing. He could smell the alcohol through the pores of his father's skin.

His voice at the carol singing was louder than anyone else's and he wouldn't stick to the tune, making his tenor slide up and down around the main notes of the song. Eileen tried to catch Jimmy's eye on the altar for a smirk but he just turned away.

The hundreds of people wishing each other a Happy Christmas as they left the church was deafening, like a roar at a football match. In the excitement their father snatched a kiss from his wife.

'Wish me happy Christmas, Maureen.'

She sighed and rested her head against the lapels of his jacket for a moment. He put Michael on his shoulders and Jimmy carried the rucksack, sharing out a bag of sweets given to him by Father Murphy, and so breathing in smog and sucking on mints. they made their way, unable to see stars or moon, wiping the particles of grime from their mouths. Back home, their father poured them all a glass of sherry and they drank the sweet, glistening liquid before going to bed and putting empty pillowcases on the floor by the beds.

Dawn came as a blast of winter sunshine through the windows dirtied with smog.

'Wake up, Eileen, wake up. Father Christmas has been.' She pushed at her sleeping sister, watching the misshapen pillow cases at the end of the old double bed.   E i l e e n rolled over to carry on sleeping. Patty pulled at the sack, putting her hand in to see what she could feel. Two oranges and a pomegranate come tumbling out. A bag of sweets and something hard like a book, a comic annual probably and then a much bigger rectangle. It was a cardboard box and she pulled back the top flap, releasing white tissue and underneath that something pink, cloudy, melting and shiny. The tissue paper fluttered to the floor as she drew out the whole dress, holding it against her, smoothing it against her chest. She buried her head in its smell of newness, the sharpness of its nylon surface rough against her nose. She didn't dare put it on yet. Some terrible superstition warned her that if she did, it might disappear, so she spreads the dress over the eiderdown above her.

'Eileen, Father Christmas brought the dress. It's lovely. It's so lovely'

Patty put her dress on for Christmas dinner. She floated downstairs in a shimmer. She was the princess off the tree. She was Grace Kelly, Rita Hayworth, Gina Lollabrigida, who met the Pope wearing a black veil, – all the beautiful women she'd ever heard of

'Give us a twirl in it now, my fairy elephant,' said her father. She leaped around the room on her sturdy legs, attempting a few Television Toppers kicks and just missing the tower built by Jimmy with his new Meccano set.

'Mind the gravy,' said her mother. 'I shouldn't be letting you wear it to dinner, but, well, just this once.'

They all helped set the table out with bowls of sprouts, parsnips and carrots, a big jug of gravy, stuffing, sausage meat and thin red crackers made from crepe paper laid next to each knife and fork. Then Mum carried in the roast turkey on a platter, amber colored and shiny.

'There you go Maureen; I told you it'd be fine. A real country turkey that. A bit over rich I admit but that's the taste of the country as I remember from my boyhood'

Despite the smell from their plates, they all picked at the vegetables and speared a bit of the dark meat.

'Mother of God,' said their mother. 'Don't eat this children. The meat is off. You'll all be sick. I'll scrape the meat off your plate. You can eat the rest of the dinner.'

'Nothing wrong with this,' said their father, continuing to chew the turkey till he spat it out on his plate.

The children watched their mother closely. They could see she was beginning to cry. May be one small tear fell down the strong bones of her face. Maybe it didn't. In later years they wouldn't remember whether she cried the Christmas with the rotten turkey or not.

'Donal Byrne, you're an idiot.' She sipped her Babycham, watching him from beneath her dark brows, her hazel eyes like candle flames.

'Yes, but I'm a good looking idiot, am I not.' He blew her a kiss from the end of the table. Michael was banging his new drum, so he picked him up and placed him on his lap and the baby pulled at the strands of sandy hair he'd shaped into a quiff, so they hung down the sides of his face.

And Patty wouldn't remember the rotten turkey at all. She'd remember the Christmas of feathers in the yard and the smoke of her floating skirt, pink and orange in the firelight.

Goebbels' House

When I saw the Wall being pulled apart on the TV news, I thought about Berlin for the first time in years. I thought of the faces of people who had once been dear to me and I thought of my father who found it difficult to forgive.

We took the tram on a hot day. I was sweating through my British Home Stores blouse and slacks and I was sure that Dieter could feel my sweating palm in his hand. We boarded the S Bahn at Zoologisches Garten. Through the smeared windows I saw Kurfurstendam and the huge Prussian buildings of the city gradually merge into suburban wooden houses and gardens bursting with soft fruit.

Our long legs flew like lances through the forest of pine, birch and oak beyond Wannsee Station, two tall teenagers with rucksacks and a small tent, one dark brown head and one red head – young, handsome and healthy.

It was cool under the trees even though the leaves were crisped burnt from the intense heat of late summer. I was a Northern English girl and not used to Eastern European weather – windless and sultry with the air hundreds of miles from a wash of sea. We stood still to listen to the drum tap of woodpeckers and then marched on, crunching fallen cones on a carpet of leaves.

We heard the shouts and laughter of swimmers in the

lake before we saw it. It cost money to enter the fenced off swimming area – there was an iron turnstile - and we had both just finished school and had no money.

'I have camped to this lake many times. Through the trees we can find other beach type place to swim.' Dieter spoke in his thick German accent which I no longer noticed. I used to think of war films but it had become so dear I didn't hear the harsh consonants and flat vowels.

We crossed the curved stone bridge onto Schwannenwerder Island, lush with olive leaved trees in the overgrown gardens of abandoned mansions. Wooden shutters hung off the windows at awkward angles. A pigeon flew out of a smashed window as we walked past. Weeds and wildflowers bent in the deeply shadowed eaves and passageways.

We found a curve of shingle and reeds. I turned my back and stripped off my blouse and slacks – to my swimsuit underneath. It felt intimate this undressing under the shade of a willow and I tugged at the bottom of my swimsuit. We held hands and walked into the lake-cold water and although the hot sun burned my white and freckled shoulders I shivered. As we swam away from the bank, the water turned from blue to brown, suddenly deepening.

We trod water and Dieter pulled me to wrap me in darkly tanned arms. I could see my legs moving like large fish through the stippled water.

'You are white, like a swan Eileen,' he said.

Only a few miles away were wooden turrets with guards holding machine guns. The border was mined and there were stories of people being blown up as they tried to escape to the West. The world was on a constant state of nuclear alert but we dissolved in one wet, river-drenched kiss in blazing sun at three in the afternoon.

We lay on our washed and washed again towels under the shade of a willow. He rested his head on one arm and looked down at me tracing the shape of my ginger brown eyebrows with his finger.

'You don't know what this island is, do you Eileen?'

'Is it something special?'

'This is where the top Nazis lived during the war. Those houses.'

'Is that why they're abandoned?'

'Well. Yes. We could sleep in one. That one over there is Goebbels' villa. I have been inside. Then we don't have to erect tent, not true?'

'Goebbels!'

'Yes, it is fine house. Not too much rubbish. We can be alone in room Eileen. Do you want that? To be with me?'

I knew all about the graded levels of sin from my religious lessons but how much I enjoyed this press of body on body. I let him touch and kiss my breasts but not beneath my swimsuit. And as he was a good boy, he didn't want to do what was not pleasing to me. As I lay beneath the willow I knew I would remember this day. I didn't know what would happen but I hungered for something.

'We could zip the sleeping bags together.' This was the most I was going to admit to. We had spent almost all the waking hours of this exchange together. His parents in their wooden house welcomed me and filled me up with German delicacies so that my willowy body was curving outwards. I did not wonder about their lives. I did not ask what Dieter's father did in the war, or his mother. I had just taken my A levels so my head was full of the couplets of Catullus, obscure, irregular French verbs and The Waste Land. The war was something that happened to my father but about which he never talked. As Dieter and his family didn't talk. Except for the Russians. Dieter's mother had talked about the Russian taking Berlin and started to weep.

The main door, of blistered wood and paint, hung on its hinges. There was a wrecked doll in the passageway, its clothes torn and dirty and a few wooden bricks. Did they belong to Geobbels' children? Nazi children. Wood pigeons coo cooed in the garden and the heavy branches of a willow rustled. Our own voices echoed in the dark hallway.

We could smell the must and damp of rooms that hadn't been lived in for decades. I could smell my own sweat and Dieter's male smell mixed with lake water. There was a crooked and cracked mirror on the wall. We looked like two swans gliding along a lake. My white blouse stuck to me now. I gripped his hand, this masculine hand with dark hairs on the back and lower joints of the fingers but he pulled away.

'I will go and find a room that is not dirty where we put our sleeping bags. Wait here.'

I kicked some litter out of the way and noticed old sheets of newspaper dated 1962, five years ago, with a photograph of President Kennedy on the front.

'Whose is all this stuff? We shouldn't be here. This is an evil place.'

'Don't you trust me? This is only time we can spend the night together, alone.'

He opened the door into a room and closed it behind us. We lowered our backpacks. He put his arm around and began to unbutton my blouse, pulling out a breast from its cotton cup and kissing it. I looked down at his short dark hair and the shape of his head bent over. Then he pulled me along the corridor into a room. It was dusk. A soft pink light floated through the windows and the sun was setting over the lake. We put down our sleeping bags on the dusty wooden floor. There was still an old key in the lock in the door so Dieter turned it.

It was so quiet. The wood pigeons in the garden: water lapping against a bank. I lit a candle. The flame cast our elongated shadows against the wall as we slipped into the sleeping bag. Dieter's hands become more daring. I began to tremble. I felt like a wild animal caught in a net. These were my secret places.

That was when we heard the footstep. Yes and another footstep moving along the hallway, outside. We stopped and looked at each other and lay still without a word, not knowing what to do, not knowing who was out there. The footsteps were close to the door. We saw the door handle being turned. Then who or whatever was out there became angry and shook the door but Dieter had locked it with an enormous rusting key.

My heart beat so fast I thought whoever was there must hear it. Dieter got out of the sleeping bag and stood still, legs apart. I reached for the candle and blew it out though my hand shook so much the hot wax spilled on my skin and on the floor. Through the window we could see the moon had risen.

The door was shaken again and we stiffened. I knew that Dieter did not know what to do. We had nothing with us to defend ourselves from whoever was out there. Was the intruder human or spirit? Did it mean us harm or was it a tramp, perhaps left over from the war who lived here? We did not say these things to each other. I made the sign of the cross and said the rosary silently on my fingers even while thinking that I was about to sin so who would listen to me?

There was a long intense waiting while we stayed rigid and silent. The door was tried one last time and then footsteps.

'Perhaps he will wait for us to come out the room.' Dieter whispered. 'Then he may attack us. Safer to stay inside.'

I nodded but my mouth could make no words. We heard a door banging far away and a motorboat on the lake but then outside we heard footsteps on the gravel.

It occurred to me that he might have looked in on us when the candle was burning. What did he want? I knew there were sadistic men. I knew how the SS had tortured people. I knew about concentration camps and gas chambers. Where was Dieter's father during the war?

'Don't be afraid Eileen. I will take care of you.'

Even in the moonlight I could see how soft his brown eyes were. He stroked my hair. We were both kids, trying on love for size for the first time. How could this tall skinny eighteen year old defend us from some larger older man who might have had a gun left from the war? But I knew he would not run away and save himself. He must have been exhausted with the effort of appearing calm and brave so he lay down beside my trembling body.

As the moon travelled its way through the sky the moonlit shadows changed angles. We waited and waited for dawn. Perhaps one of us fitfully fell asleep. Gradually the room began to fill with grey light. A blackbird sang its passionate song in the garden. Strangely I wondered whether Mutti would have made us more plum cake last night. And then I thought of the border guards up in their turrets turning to face over the wall into the West. The light became rosier and warmer. I knew that we would be able to leave the room soon. I wondered where the intruder was now. Was he hiding in undergrowth in the woods? Was there a cellar, a bunker left from the War?

As soon as the sky became blue Dieter unlocked the door ever so quietly and holding my hand we ran with all of our youth out through this hallway and out through the broken door and along the road onto the bridge back to home singing and shouting.

What You Need For Happiness

Not much when
You think about it
Two people
A bottle of wine
A little cheese
Salt, bread
A room
Window and door
The rain outside
Long stems of rain
And, of course, cigarettes

(From poem of the same title by Peter Kanto 'The Colonnade of Teeth, Modern Hungarian Poetry', Bloodaxe, 1996)

It's what she's always imagined living in when she was poorer, Edwardian terrace, a street of plane and cherry trees, large bay windows, canopies over the doors, a turret here and there, picture rails and dados, fireplaces with pretty tiles. The front door is heavy and slightly warped, painted ochre yellow. A man of about seventy opens the door. His thick, grey hair is brushed back from an angled forehead; his cheekbones jut and the brown eyes sit deep in shadow. His short-sleeved shirt is tucked into trousers, belted under his stomach. 'Come in Mrs. Thompson. Welcome,' he says, offering a tanned hand. He takes her into the sitting room when she is offered a chair with bright cushions, embroidered with flowers. Along the back of the sofa lie white cotton runners, threaded with scarlet. The heavy leaves of a plant in a brass dish brush against her arm. Two rooms have been knocked through to make this long sitting room but the opening is badly finished. The strangest feature is the bar in the corner. It is made of bronzed Formica and is edged in gilt. The sides ripple in rows of flattened pipes. On the shelves behind the bar are soda siphons, toothpicks in wooden egg-cups, jars of cherries and some small flags with red, white and green stripes.

He shows her the kitchen which is covered in strips of wood, like a sauna, but a few strips have peeled away from the wall. There is a wood-burning stove in the corner and resting on it a large enamel tureen, hanging by three chains from a stand.

'This is my soup tureen. Fish soup is a speciality of my home town.' He offers a smile that turns up the curve of his mouth but does not show his teeth.

'Sounds exotic.' She presses her lips together, embarrassed that she does not know about fish soup.

'Would you like a drink, Mrs. Thompson?' He lifts a bottle of vodka off the shelf and waves it gently in the air.

'Joan, please. But at eleven in the morning, no thanks.' Lonely, old man, she thinks. She continues with the usual questions about wiring, heating and neighbours.

'I did the plumbing myself,' he says with a grin. 'I'm an engineer.'

She goes back for a second viewing. The house will mean

a big hike in the mortgage but she longs to move into this part of Middlesbrough, Linthorpe, with its gracious, old houses, leafy avenues, newsagents that sell The Guardian, left-of-centre barbecues. She's slaved for this.

She's put on foundation and a nice sienna lipstick that suits her auburn hair. She slips on heels, hoping this won't make her taller than Mr. Sandor.

The sun's streaming through the heavy, lace curtains in the bay when she arrives. She looks at the photos on the mantelpiece, one of a young man at graduation, a wedding, a good looking couple in their thirties, two girls in primary school uniforms. She sees at the back a faded black and white photo of a beautiful, fine-featured face, framed by thick waving hair. The woman's chin rests on a long-fingered hand.

'Family photos, Mr. Sandor?'

'That is George, my son who works in London and that is Stephen who works in Canada. The grandchildren there are George's.'

Joan points at the old photograph. 'Is that your wife? She was very beautiful.'

He sighs. 'That's the girl I left behind in Hungary in 1956, nearly fifty years ago.'

'I've heard of the uprising, but I was a tiny baby then.'

'I evaded the border guards and walked into Austria on a tree trunk that had fallen across a river. And I ended up here. It's a long story.'

He tells her to look around the house by herself so she trails upstairs, stopping by the bookshelves on the landing with their Hungarian titles. Decorated gourds sit on the top shelf. When she's come downstairs he's poured himself a drink.

'Have some barak. It's a kind of apricot schnapps.'

She sips the fiery liquid. It burns her throat. She knows she shouldn't do this, she should speak to the estate agent but he looks so approachable.

'Where are you moving to?'

He lights a cigarette. 'That's another long story.'

'You're a taciturn man.'

'We don't tell strangers our business in Hungary.'

'You're not in Hungary and I'm not a stranger. I might be living in your house.' She clinks glasses with him.

'I brought my family up here. My boys went to the school around the corner and my wife used to help there. She was English.'

'Mr. Sandor.'

'Call me Laszlo.'

'I'd like to make an offer but I'd have to get a lot of work done on it. The decorations and so on are not modern.'

'You're not from round here, are you, Joan. You don't have the accent.'

'No, I'm a Londoner.'

'And?'

'I came here with two small children to get away from a violent husband. It wasn't easy. I worked hard, sometimes at two jobs. Now they're grown up I want to live somewhere nice. I've always loved these streets. I met a woman who lived here at a party, once. At that time I was poor and desperate. When I saw her a few days later she crossed to the other side of the street so she wouldn't have to talk to me.'

'At least she wasn't going to report you to the AVH.'

'Sorry?'

'The secret police of the communist era.'

'Ah.'

'It's a shame to talk business with such an attractive woman.' He leans to refill her glass. She smoothes the skirt of her dress over her slim legs. The attention feels nice.

'I can offer you £10,000 below the asking price.'

'But Joan, I need everything I can get to arrange things. I will buy a small flat near my son and a house in Hungary. You see I am going back for a long visit once the house is sold..'

The drink has relaxed her into her natural good humour. 'Are you going to look for your lost love?'

'You have a romantic imagination. Perhaps. England has been my life. I married a nice, jolly English woman and we lived a good life. This was the centre for the Hungarian Association here.'

She looks into her glass, wondering what to say, thinking that perhaps she has asked too much. He stands and looks down at her.

'Are you buying this on your own?'

She is aware of his gaze on the flow of skirt over her thighs and silver earrings, glittering in the sunshine as she speaks. She brushes a strand of hair behind her ear.

'Since I ran away from London I have more or less avoided getting involved with anyone and I was so busy working and bringing up children. I really like this house. There is a warm atmosphere here.'

'We had a lot of fun in this sitting room. Parties, Christmases, visitors. I do not like aggression. I feel a sense of growing older but also full of possibility. '

'The streets where I live have got edgy. Fights, drug deals on the corner, people drifting in and out. I want to live somewhere peaceful where people leave out saucers of milk for hedgehogs.'

He tells her that they should leave this business to the estate agents, as that is what they are paid to do. She enjoys the fact that he really listens to her when she talks, leaning forward on his chair. He wants to know how she earns her living and tells her about how he was sent to Teesside as a refugee when he first arrived in England.

'I came at the right time when the steel industry was expanding. There was work. But now, where are the jobs?

Maybe some jobs have even moved to Hungary, although even there they don't mine coal anymore.'

She leaves her phone number with him in case he wants to discuss the offer. She feels tipsy, schnapps in the heat have gone straight to her head and she totters in her heels to the corner, aware of a pair of brown eyes watching. How can a man of seventy have such amused, sparkling eyes?

She thinks he might phone and he does, asking her if she'd like to go for a meal, as eating alone is so melancholy. Would it be like having lunch with her father, she wonders, well he's not quite old enough for that. She thinks of her life full of swimming and walks, the friends, the book club, the children who visit from time to time but there is still an ache she has learned to live with.

He opens the car door to let her in and helps her out of the car, pours her drinks. Over lunch he becomes more expansive. She has put on dark trousers and a red cotton shirt that suits her hair colour. Not too glamorous she thinks. She still hasn't had a response from the estate agents. This is like fraternising with the enemy, she smiles, but he's not her enemy. He's a charming, older man who likes good food and wine and Russian cigarettes – the only thing Russian he likes.

They disagree about politics but talk about gardening and films which they both love. She takes the vegetarian option which he teases her about. He orders a steak, to be served rare.

'We are both survivors of kinds of war,' he says over coffee. 'Not that either of us are heroes, I expect.'

She agrees, thinking about the refuge she hid in, the years of making ends meet and further back her own difficult relationship with her step-mother.

'Yes,' he draws on his Sobranie. 'The fragmented family. I tried not to do that. In Hungary I might have had a mistress it might have been accepted. But here, instant divorce. I didn't want that.'

She wonders if that is some kind of invitation and asks him about his story, whether he has ever regretted coming here.

'No, this country welcomed me when I was desperate. And why? We weren't their allies during the war, though of course, Cold War politics altered who was friends with who. When I was first sent to Teesside from the refugee centre in London, I was shocked by the poverty. We believed that in the West people must live much better than us but here I found people jobless, living in mean conditions, in cold houses and eating badly. But people were kind. And I was from a rural part of Hungary myself so why should I object to being sent to the far north. We were put in a hostel and there was some trouble with local men. The girls liked us you see. Hungarian men know how to be charming to a woman.' He laughs and taps her hand on the table.

'Why didn't you come with your girlfriend?'

'I am not proud to tell you that she got injured in the uprising and I wanted desperately to get out. I told you, I was not a hero. There I've said it.'

'Is that why you want to go back, to make up for things?'

He kisses her hand and tells her it is time for him to drop her home. No-one has done that before and she feels flattered and amused. He drops her outside her town house, its windows sparkling and its brass knocker shining in the dusk sunlight. She wonders if she should ask him in but feels a sense of panic. What if he assumes that is an invitation for an affair. He looks strong. He would know how to make her feel sensuous, she knows this. He would be grateful to her but for God's sake she's trying to buy his house at a good price! She gives a little wave and disappears inside. His dark eyes seem to glitter through the car window. Amusement or disappointment, she's not sure.

The estate agent phones a few days later. The vendor cannot accept the offer as it stands. Perhaps she should think about increasing it? Perhaps a compromise could be reached. There are other, similar houses she could view, though. Damn, she thinks, well he's not soft enough to drop what he wants because we shared a bottle of wine and an expensive meal. I'll offer a bit more, she decides.

On Friday evening he phones again to invite her to a fund-raising dance at the Masonic Lodge. 'You know, the one on Roman Rd. But perhaps the music would be a little old-fashioned for you?' he asks.

'I don't know how to dance those kinds of dances, like quickstep and foxtrot.'

'Oh, a deprived childhood, I see. Well, let me make up for it. I lead, you follow.'

'Mmm. Well I could go, out of kindness to an old man.' She pauses, thinking, Damn, I shouldn't have said that, it's too rude, and then she hears him laughing.

'The coach and horses will collect you at seven thirty tomorrow.'

He hoots outside, leaning over to open the door for her. She slides herself into the seat of his Mazda in her one expensive dress, fine, apricot wool, tight across the body. It accentuates her curves but it's hardly a ball-gown.

'You look sophisticated. I'm so glad you're not wearing an over the top, English-woman ball-gown. It makes them look like Viennese cakes.' He kisses her right hand and doesn't let go but starts driving, holding on to it.

'I'm not very good with strangers,' she says. 'I don't know how to make small talk.'

'I've noticed. Don't worry, you'll have a few dances, eat some not bad food and have a few drinks. Nothing to get excited about. We could all do with a little fun.'

It's a live band, strictly tempo. There can't be a musician in it below sixty but they play flawlessly and he quicksteps to the rhythm. There are a few stumbles and he has to pull her to him to keep her steady. She can smell cigarette smoke and aftershave, something spicy and expensive. He doesn't seem to have any aches and pains, gliding about the floor in his shiny, leather shoes. She wonders, don't older people have aches and pains?

Surprisingly there are a few faces she recognises, some connected to the Job Centre where she works and so she chats in the Ladies with Alma while she renews her sienna lipstick and blots the sweat off her face with toilet paper.

'That was fun,' she turns to him as the car swings into Linthorpe Rd and the streams of young people heading into the town's clubs pass by.

'Glad you enjoyed it. Your dancing got better with each song.'

She's not sure if she's attracted to him or not. He's so much older, another generation. But his wit and confidence are pulling down the barbed wire.

'Laszlo, it's ages since I had fun like that – though it's not the kind of thing I usually go do. A fund-raising do for the Labour Party is more my fancy night out, you know, cheap Chardonnay and real ale and earnest conversations.'

'Sounds dull. I like pleasure – good food, laughter, holidays, good books and films. I had enough of politics in the past.' He stops the car and leans over to kiss her, an experienced, unhurried and sensuous kiss, like sipping brandy in the foyer of The Ritz.

'I like you Joan,' he says, holding her face, his signet ring cutting into her cheek. 'We could have some nice times together. You could do with some easy pleasure. You life is full of busy things that you take too seriously. My wife was sick for a long time before she died. I'm not too old to feel desire, love even.'

Yes, she thinks, the schedule of each week to fit everything in, the plans and lists. Yes, maybe a little Hungarian barak and indolent Sundays would not go amiss.

'What about the house? I want it so much. I've worked two jobs for it. Overtime. No holidays. And what about the lost love in Hungary?'

'Let the house take care of itself. The estate agents will see to that. Let's do something spontaneous and get the train from Darlington tomorrow to link up with the Eurostar to Paris. Zsuzsa? I don't even know if she is still alive, and,' he strokes the inside of her arm. 'This is skin, warm, soft and breathing.'

The rain is falling and the lights of Linthorpe Rod dissolve into greasy raindrops on his windscreen so that the blues, reds, ambers and greens blur and melt like oil paint.

'Well, just a weekend,' she says. 'I'm not going to look after you in your dotage.'

Oasis

Our laughter sizzled like lightly frying chilies.

'Well, I told him I've got four children and a weight problem and he just smiled and said – a real African woman.'

'Did you tell him you dilute your coke with vodka on good days?'

Cecilia grinned. 'And secret tabs.' She pulled a packet of Regals out of one of the pockets of her red cotton tabard.

'I thought you'd given up since meeting Karimu?'

'You won't let on will you?'

We sat in the back yard of my house in Palm St. The sun was going down at the end of the rows of terraced houses. A town on fire. Sun flames over the gridiron of streets. Light washed over the bricks, glinting on the leaves of the honeysuckle I had growing in tubs. It had reached the broken glass on the top of the next door neighbour's wall. A blackbird ululated from a chimney, its song like a chandelier glistening in a shabby house.

We'd been neighbours for fifteen years; had watched over each other's children. She still had younger ones longing to grow up. They were battered by the war that had raged between their parents. Attack, retreat, resistance, ambush. A defeat. Col could be cruel. He could be violent. He'd been driven out.

Her girls had inherited the mud-brown eyes, flecked with amber. Her wide-boned, diamond shaped face. They were different shades of vanilla and caramel. Pretty as. But none of them had her Afro hair that was pulled into a knot at the back. She laughed as she told me about Karimu, the pizza delivery man.

'Sometimes he looks at me, like, it's in a cartoon, little hearts shooting out of his eyes. He just delivered the pizzas I'd ordered and look what happened!'

She'd been through a lot. The ex not only smashing up the house when drunk but using racist abuse, – her, the mother of his four children. If he did that was he not cursing his own children? Surely his life would rot after.

The brickwork was cooling down. From the attic window you could see the Transporter glinting in the sunset like a huge Victorian brass bed over a beaten copper river. Below, the urgent flames of industry shouted money, work, muck.

This town was made of migrants. A hundred fifty years ago it had been a gold rush town, male, with ten men to every woman. Men came to dig out iron, turn iron ore into steel, build ships with the steel, build docks for the ships and houses for the workers. Men walked from Wales and Scotland. In the farms of Ireland men kissed their mothers and sweethearts goodbye. There were roads, factories, town halls, hospitals and schools to be built.

Women followed. Women down on their uppers, women

in want of a husband, women on the make. Some men married local girls or girls who'd drifted here. Some brought their girls with them. Some sent for girls from back home. A few probably had two wives – one here and one there.

Later men jumped ship from far flung parts of the world, like Somalia or Yemen or Algeria.

Can anyone really say where one tribe ends and another begins? People have always loved across borders. Nomads wandering across the desert don't always move in search of the best grazing. A woman fetching water at a well, sees a pair of eyes burning her. She uses all her guile to get the caravan to move back to that oasis. Hunger to see that face again. The heart can row you across an ocean. The heart is a refugee with one cardboard suitcase packed with all the hope it owns.

Or you can change life on a whim. To prove someone wrong. To show you account for something. Boys hide in ships from Liberia, in airplanes from India. Maybe they'll survive. Maybe they won't. All your chips on one number.

Cecilia's mother had married a seaman from Nigeria and her family turned against her, so that her children didn't meet their English grandparents until they made their first holy communion. Her father, who always wore a suit, worked in the docks and her mother at the greengrocers. There had never been enough money to visit Nigeria, so Cecilia knew it only from her father's stories and the few photographs he had of his mother in the village.

'Have the kids met Karimu yet?' I asked her. We were finishing off the last of the vodka and coke.

'No. Not yet. We need to do things decently. I've only just got the courts to banish Col from coming within a mile of the house. Karimu wants to marry me. To marry me! With four children. '

'It's those eyes of yours. It must be. It can't be the bank balance.'

'He needs to do this to get his papers. Time's running out. He says there's no future at home but he swears he loves me and wants to be with me but I know he needs the papers. I've just got out of one terrible mess so I can't jump into another.'

We lit our Regals and blew smoke against the gnats. We'd shared so many drinks in the past, talking through our messy lives till the truth was cold and transparent as ice in vodka.

She told me how she'd gone into her first marriage, full of hope that it would last like her parents. Never a cross word between them, she told me and at first things had been happy but, with time, Col's drinking got worse. Losing his job, merchandising on the ships in port, hadn't helped. Their life unravelled like a jumper snagged on a nail.

A few months later as I was cleaning the front step I saw the pizza van, with its basket of vegetables painted on the side, pull up outside the house. The children tumbled out the back with sandy feet and buckets. Karimu waved to me.

'Just back from Saltburn. I'm barbecuing some children in the back. Come round later.' He giggled as he went into the house, shouting. 'I know you English think we're cannibals who live in trees,' and he gnashed his teeth at me.

Smoke and flames rose from the charcoal he was fanning with a copy of the local Gazette. Cecilia brought me a beer. Her hair was in dozens of tight braids with a small bright bead at the base of each one.

'Cool hairstyle,' I said.

'Aisha, sat out there, did it for me. She's from Ghana. She says all African girls learn how to do it from their mothers. Mum didn't know what to do with our hair, so now I'm learning. Mum just wanted a happy home. She wasn't interested in trying to be more African than an African.'

Karimu walked through and patted her on the backside. He wasn't much taller than her but powerfully built, with deep frown lines. You wouldn't describe him as handsome but his eyes drew you in, as he looked so closely at everything. He was quite solemn, not smiling much but had an occasional, soft, beguiling laugh. And he always dressed formally, often wearing the same dark red jacket, white shirt, tie, black trousers and polished shoes.

In the kitchen he seemed more relaxed, turning over pieces of seasoning chicken. The smell of garlic, basil, chili, onion and ginger gave an exotic perfume that I was beginning to appreciate. All these things for sale now in the Asian shops.

Cecilia and I loved pottering there, exulting in the trays of mysterious vegetables and packets of spices.

He opened his beer with strong, square teeth, wiping the rim on a tea towel and told me he'd make an African woman out of Cecilia, surprised she knew so little about her father's culture. ' She could give me a child. It's not too late,' he said.

I explained that I was third generation Irish, my grandfather having travelled from a farm in Monaghan to work in the building trade. And then I asked him how he had ended up in Middlesbrough. It was a story of dangerous journeys, risk taking. He'd needed to leave his home area because it had been destroyed by the oil companies. He had walked across a good bit of the Sahara.

'Walked? That's impossible.'

'No. Just difficult. It took months. We paid Tuareg guides to take us from one small oasis to the next. We walked early morning and at night, carrying water and a little food. We sheltered where we could.' He told me a little more about Libya and working there and boats to Italy. I couldn't imagine how much courage and determination all that would need and I could only shake my head in astonishment.

The children ran in and out the narrow yard, laughing for the first time in a long time, excited at having guests and noisy conversation. When all the chicken was eaten, the moon rose over the town, a fat, pumpkin moon, bringing with it cool air off the North Sea onto the simmering tarmac. A police siren yawped nearby. A can was kicked along a pavement outside. Bhangra music blasted out of a car racing past. Karimu tapped a rhythm on an upturned saucepan and Aisha sang a plaintive song. Then I said I'd sing something Irish I'd learnt from my grandfather – The Croppy Boy. I could see the faces of the young children of the Pakistani family next door pressed against their bedroom window watching, mouths open. Cecilia sat her ample self on Karimu's knee and they giggled softly like teenagers.

A few weeks later on my way to work I saw the pizza van was parked outside and all four tyres spreading on the tarmac, slashed.

'It was Col wasn't it?' I said to Cecilia as we pushed our trolleys around Kwiksave.

'Yeah, he must've heard from a neighbour. Or saw us together. The fact that he's a real African. He won't like that.'

'Mad bastard.'

'I won't let him spoil things for me. I stood up to him when I was alone. Karimu would deal with him if I told him the address.'

'Then he'd get done. Col would get a gang of mates with baseball bats, if he has any, mates that is, or the police would be called and he'd get deported.'

'He's lost his job. He shouldn't have been working without papers and the pizza shop can't claim on the insurance.'

She reached up to get some tins of beans and turned

round with that look she gets when she's made her mind up about something. It's like a gas flame being lit.

'To hell with him! I'll marry Karimu. Then he won't have to be looking over his shoulder all the time. He wants to work hard and start a business.'

'But Cecilia, what if he's got a wife in Africa already? How do you know he's telling the truth? And what about the kids? How do you know he'll be good to them?'

She bit her lip and tossed back her braids. 'Well, he wouldn't be the first to have two wives, let's face it. No, he wouldn't be the first to do that. If he has a wife back home, well who knows, maybe we'll send her some money to help her out. I'm not a jealous woman.' Her laughter got swallowed by the boy racers down Linthorpe Rd.

'And the children? They like it that he's good to me. Kids are not stupid. Like me, they want some peace and kindness.'

They married in the register office by the Bottle of Notes. She ordered the yellow dress and matching slingbacks for the wedding, from my catalogue. Before the karaoke started at the reception, the eldest boy made a speech welcoming Karimu into the family. Everyone was crying, even the barmaid, wiping her face with a tea towel. For old time's sake, I bought Cecilia a vodka and coke and we clinked glasses.

'Go easy on the vodka,' I said. 'This is your wedding day.'

Odelia

I check my red nails and pull my top down over my jeans, wiggling in the seat because they too tight, cut in. A strand of hair falls over my face and I smell it for tobacco. Mr. Bill doesn't like the smell. My denim knees nearly touch the knees of man in blue suit opposite.

Each stop take us further away from city and door whinges as opens and shuts. The train judders off throwing my knees against wool knees. He even risks a smile – in that Englishman way, not really a smile, like has machine inside mouth pushing mouth wider. I look at him sideways so he can't see I looking at him. That's how we do it in my country. I see him looking me over. Must be pretty today.

Sun is shining for one time so I look out of windows and outside it greener, bushier, lots of trees, leaves – like in rainy season at home. Sunlight on the green. Not grey, not dark like in winter. That was hard. If Sabrina did not give me her old coat and jumper, I die, oh. But I still here though they close in on me. It getting harder. Only nice lady in the church find me cleaning work.

Blue suit gets up to go. Looks at me. Handsome young man. Must take his nice suit to good job. Door groans again, slides back cutting off nice man. But I do not find young man to take care of me, give me papers – they too suspicious. Sabrina says I must try get Mr. Bill to like me.

I flex out my fingers. Strong, rough hands from all that cleaning. And strong slim back from all that up and down stairs and windows. If my mother could see how I clean! But I don't tell her what I do when I call. This only make her sad and the line crackly so. I don't tell her how I look out – always in case police notice me. Then I know what happens. It happen to friends before.

Few minutes till I get there and then I see something green flying. It stop on a branch. Big green bird. My God, a parrot! Must be escaped from someone's house. Must be happy to be free. It flies to different tree. It watch as we rattle by. How will it last winter? It's free but, survive? I don't expect parrot in far North where they send me. Maybe it brings good luck. I check my bag – yes I have cream, scarf and those pills – so much money I pay for them. Sabrina tells me they make Mr. Bill fall in love with me, like potion you get from wise woman back home.

When I get off I smell sea air, fresh, clean. It nice here. Big houses – everything smart, fancy, flowers in garden. My heels clop clop on the pavement to Mr. Bill. I shake inside. Must not show it. This is only way. I swing hips down street till I get to red door and bang brass lion, looking dull. I will polish today.

He pleased to see me when he open door. Lonely old man. The hallway full of big, heavy pictures – mountains and some kind of gazelle. Hard to reach for dusting. When door shuts the sound from the street cut off. His house always so quiet except when he has TV on very very loud. I always start with sitting room. It is crowded with dark furniture.

'You want me start in here Mr. Bill?' I say

'Kitchen needs going over a bit, Odelia, if you don't mind.' And he stays in sitting room to read paper while I get out the hoover and dusters, put on plastic gloves and fast fast wipe all the surface and tidy away jams and pots. I spray sink and bleach it. I mop the tile floor in swishy movement. Tiles all shining now, like dark red lipstick.

'Cup of tea Mr. Bill?' I shout.

'That would be lovely my dear.' He always like that I sit drink tea with him after kitchen cleaned. I get the packet of tablets out of my handbag. I stop. My hand shake. I'm not good time girl. But I so desperate. In my heart I say I am sorry to whoever listening. Drop in one blue tablet and two spoonful sugar and stir. I rinse spoon and put on draining board.

I carry mugs on tray into sitting room. Mr Bill smiles and reaches for tea.

'Another soldier killed today,' he looks up. 'I don't know where this will end.'

'Poor people who live there,' I say. I know what it is to live in war zone. I remember so many things that I never talk about. But I was very young then.

'Poor buggers.' He drinks his tea with big sucking noises.

I pull the pouf.

'I do feet today Mr. Bill?' and I lift his feet onto pouf and untie laces, taking off shiny, brown shoes with little pattern and woolly, brown socks. I roll up corduroy trouser legs and sit on squashy pouf, one foot on my lap. Skin very dry and nails need cutting.

'You want nails trim, Mr. Bill?' I smile up at him. He nods, pleased. I take out clipper from pocket and snip all wide, thick edges like starched shirt collar. Then I rub Intensive Care cream onto my hands and smooth into foot starting with ankle, then arch and sole. I stretch toes one by one and rub circles at base. I make circles on sole of foot. Mr. Bill's head goes back and his face dreamy oh. When both feet done and lying on my lap I trace shape of heart with my finger on the front.

'You do that very well Odelia. No one ever touches old people.' He looks sad.

'You not really old Mr. Bill – just a bit old. Plenty of life.'

'No-one to do life with now my Jeannie is gone.'

I reach over and pat his hand but he puts his other hand on top and squeezes. I stay very still but nothing more happen.

'Must go and finish clean house now,' I say as I swing out . I get hoover and bang it over carpet, move armchair back and coffee table. It roar back and forward as I bend to move things and to turn up and down power. Mr. Bill sit and watch me. He not reading newspaper now. I know I have nice shape, slim legs. I turn round fast and see him looking and smile. His papery skin go red colour and he looks down at paper. I polish furniture with spray and wipe all photos. His daughter and grandchildren look out from boat, all smiles and blonde hair. Also photo of woman, old like Bill. Nice smile. Short white hair and glasses.

'I do upstairs now,' I say and carry machine up stairs with cloth and spray. I sing as I work, songs from home, new song I hear on radio, There Goes My Baby, with nice tune.

When I finish I shout down

'Mr. Bill please can I have bath before I clean bathroom. Water heater broke where I live.' He comes out into hallway and looks up stairs, cross face.

'Well I suppose so.'

I run water into bath and smell soap. Imperial leather. Man soap. Spice smell. All of me fit in bath stretched out, my head against curve. I soap my body from feet to face. I rub myself dry with blue towel. His wife buy good things, quality – big soft towels, thick white cotton sheets.

I think maybe I should go down in towel and see what happen. But maybe this frighten him. Not good idea. I put back yellow top and jeans and run fingers through hair. Then I wipe everything so all shiny and white surface on bath, sink, ledge and shelf. Then I go down stairs and put all cloth, spray, hoover away in big cupboard under stairs.

I go into the sitting room. He is looking out of front window.

'Garden very pretty now Mr. Bill. All those flowers.'

'Yes, it's been a good summer. The roses have blossomed. Would you like me to cut you some to take home?'

'Oh yes,' I say. We go out to garden together and he snip red ones, then orange and white and bunch them. The sun slants on my face and on the windows.

'Let me wrap them in some paper,' he says and goes inside. I follow him into kitchen where he takes sheets of newspaper and rolls the flowers inside. Scent fills air and I breathe in.

'Roses for a beautiful lady,' he says as he presses them into my arms.

'No one else gives me flowers.'

He looks at me with his pale eyes.

'No boyfriend Odelia?'

'I have no one. Just my mother, so far away, back home. She look after my daughter.' I look up at him and I am just lifting my arm to put on his shoulder when he reach into his pocket for cash and pulls out twenty pound note and press this into my hand. I think pill must not work. What can I do?

'Mr. Bill. Thankyou.' I bite my lip. I want to say but cannot find word. Then it comes to me.

'It nice evening Mr. Bill. You like to walk with me by sea?'

He stands silent. The grandfather clock bongs loud in

front room. I hear children scream and chase in next door house.

'Well. Why not?'

I help him into jacket and we walk down street and cross over to path near beach. The light all pretty, pink and mauve and the sea like milk. Boats with white triangles sail on water. The beach still full of people. The shouting and laughter echo as they pick up bags and climb the steps up. Big sea birds stop on pavement near by, fold their white white wings, like bleached cotton. No sign of parrot.

Then we sit down on bench. Big boats far far away across the sea. I see lights come on along boat as it get dark a bit. Little noisy boats like scooter zip across the sea.

I move in bit close to Bill so he can smell nice, clean Imperial Leather smell. I am bold. I put my bare arm through his. He look round surprise but with other hand he stroke skin of arm. I pretend like I not notice. I feel his fingers on arm move up and down. He do it like he never stop. I shiver.

'Are you getting cold Odelia? Maybe we should go back.'

'You not hungry Mr. Bill?' He buys fish and chips. We sit on bench and share but wind make chips cold quick quick.

'Here nice piece of fish Mr. Bill.' And I hold up white flesh to his mouth and push in to feed him.

Once the front door close I help him off with jacket and stand very close.

'You nice man Mr. Bill,' I whisper. I slip shoulder out of

Odelia

t shirt so lot of skin show. He make small animal noise, like he in pain. He put hands to head. I invite with eyes. But then silence and nothing.

'Odelia - I was a soldier in Malaya when I was young. I am a man of the world.' A man is a man and wants to taste the fruit so he reach for me. Then phone rings.

'Leave it Mr Bill,' I say but he shake head and go into sitting room. Because phone turned up to loudspeaker I hear woman voice at other end – 'Hello Daddy.' And I know is the woman in the photograph. I pull up t shirt strap and go into kitchen, put on kettle and sit down swinging my leg cross over. I hear him say he go for walk to beach but not say with me. Hmm. Yes daughter not like this my arrangement.

I find bottle of whisky in cupboard so I make tea and pour in dash and when phone call finish I take in to Mr. Bill. He turn and look at me as I come in like he is working out puzzle, putting bits together. I sit on arm of chair and put his tea on small table.

He pick up tea and sit on sofa.

'Best if you go home Odelia after you finish your tea.'

I give small sigh. One tablet not enough.

I fetch my bag and stand before Mr. Bill and say

'I going home now Mr. Bill. If you want. '

'Yes.'

The lion bangs when I close door and clop clop back to

metro. But I turn right to go to seafront and I sit on bench looking out to sea. I wonder how many weeks on boat it take to get home. Must be nice I think. All that sky and ocean and stars at night. The stars come out now. I see one sad moon face over sea.

As I walk to station I hear train noise coming so I clop clop faster. I don't know what time it is. But I think must be late. I hear train groan into station but my heels too high and I cannot run. When I reach platform, doors close. I try pressing button but mean driver pull train out of station. The lights of the last metro curve away from the platform, leave Station silent.

I breathe heavy. Taxi cost all cash I just make. What to do? I walk slowly back and knock lion again. I hear television through window. Mr. Bill have it very loud. I knock again more times. I see Mr. Bill pull back heavy curtain. Then I wait. He open door just a little.

'Mr. Bill I miss last train. I cannot get home.' Poor Mr. Bill, he frowns and shake head but he too kind to leave me on street. The night cold now and the city full of bad people. I go in and take off my shoes.

Kaya

The moon made the ocean silvery and the plane flipped so low we seemed to be just above the tops of forest trees. Then we had a noisy landing with the brakes screeching but everyone in the plane clapped. Dad pulled my rucksack out of the overhead cupboard and asked me if I was OK.

'We're home,' he said.

But it wasn't my home. That was back in England, in 45 Willowbay Rd. Dad stood for ages in front of me at the top of the metal stairs, just breathing in, and the other passengers were laughing at him. But when I got through the plane door I could smell that flowery smell in the air and the heat was like being wrapped in a duvet

The airport was tiny but full of noise and people. Everyone was shouting and pushing, so Dad told me to stand close to the passport control, while he went to get the big suitcase, and it really was big, the size of a fridge.

The lights from the airport were the only lights around, so the streets were really dark. I could see the faces of the big boys hanging around outside, because they were lit up from that yellow inside light coming through the windows.

The bus took us to a dock where a big ferry was waiting and we drove inside. Dad said it was too hot to stay there, so we got out and pushed our way through the crowds of people on the stairs and passages. Dad took my hand and told me to watch my rucksack. He bought me a coke in a café and there were two comedians telling jokes, one with a painted, white face but I couldn't understand what they were saying. Dad said they were making fun of people like him, coming back, 'justcams'. He took me outside to look at the sky and the river. It was so wide you couldn't see the city on the other side and the black water was swirling around and slapping against the sides of the old ferry. Dad told me it was opening out into the Atlantic and I could see, by the moonlight, the edge of the land and beyond, where the ocean was.

'This is where they carried the slaves from,' he said. 'There's an island way up there where they held them.'

I kept that information. Dad liked to know that I would remember things like that.

I looked at the moonshine on the water and thought about Mum. She wouldn't have liked this crowded ship, I know. I missed her so much but Dad got annoyed if I kept asking when she was coming back or if she was coming to meet us here, so I didn't say anything. We had to push out way back to the bus again for landing and I squashed against a girl my age, putting a bowl of something on her head. Our eyes met and she looked at my long braids with the beads at the end that clanked in the wind. Dad had let me get it done before we travelled. Her hair was corn-rowed to her scalp in segments.

Dad said the bus would drop us in Rawdon St and that his

cousin would be there to pick us up. It seemed a long way from the dock, with no street lights, just small lamps by the sides of stalls but the pavements were full of people walking in the dark. We got off outside a shop and Dad told me to look down as we walked to the bottom of the slope, because of the broken pavements and open drains. It didn't smell nice. Everyone was black, you know, really black, like Daddy. I didn't see one white person apart from a woman in a big car, who leaned out of the window to buy eggplants from a stall.

Dad's cousin came to meet us in a taxi, a yellow one. We all squashed in on the torn seats. The driver turned the steering wheel with a wad of notes in his hand. Dad and Uncle Bockarie talked and laughed the whole way, but I couldn't understand what they were saying. Dad had taught me some Krio and spoke to me sometimes but Mummy didn't really like it. What's the point of teaching her that language, she would say. Uncle Bockarie turned to me and touched my cheek.

'So this is Natasha. Fine girl. Welcome.'

I didn't know what to say so I just pressed my hands onto my jeans and smiled. The taxi had to stop sometimes because the road was very busy and boys came with newspapers, pushing them into the window but Uncle Bockarie just waved them away.

We stopped outside a yellow house, with a metal gate that swung open into a yard. A small, fat woman with a blue scarf tied around her head stood there and I knew it was grandma, because I'd seen her in photographs. She put her arms around me and pulled me against her bosom, which was hard and squashy at the same time and I could smell cooking on her, a sort of oniony, spicy smell.

'So na u na mi bobo im pikin, Thank God I don finally see you.'

She was nice and warm and I liked her fat arms around me. Dad was smiling looking at us. And then there was a whole heap of grown-ups and kids crowding around, but Dad told everyone to go inside, where we all perched on the chairs and edges of chairs in the sitting room. On the blue wall there were lots of photos of me and Dad and one of Mummy and Dad's wedding day but later Dad took down that photo because I never saw it again. In the photo Mummy was wearing a long white dress and her blonde hair was done in a knot with flowers.

Grandma brought me a bottle of Seven Up from a big freezer in the corner. It was nice and cold and I was so hot in my jeans and sweatshirt and socks and trainers. My cousins were chattering away to me and laughing. Jocelyn, who was about my age, brought me a plate of rice and stew from the back. It was spicier than how Dad cooks it but I tried to finish it. They put the television on and it was a music programme, so what with all the music and chatting, hot food and smell of the diesel from the generator, I felt quite dizzy. I wondered what Dad was doing. And where the toilet was.

Kaya

Grandma came out to sit with me.

'A big girl,' she said squashing in next to me. 'How you do in school?'

'I'm learning the viola, grandma.' She smiled but I was sure she didn't know what that was because Dad hadn't till I explained it to him. I didn't know whether to call her Grandma Claudia because I had another Grandma in Poland, Grandma Danuta, who I had met.

At last Dad came back and leaned over me.

'Now then Tasha, you will sleep with Grandma in the big double bed and I'll be down the hallway. I've got a mosquito net to fix up over the bed. And take your tablets with your drink. Don't drink the water. Grandma will boil some up and keep it in the fridge for you. Jocelyn, take Tasha to the bathroom so she knows where the toilet is.'

Sleeping with Grandma! I've got my own room, at home, with a TV in it.

Jocelyn took me down the corridor to the back. It was a proper toilet, like back home. I'd been worried it wouldn't be. She told me to take water from the bucket of water standing in the bath to wash my hands, as the taps didn't work.

Although it was so hot and noisy outside, as I could hear the men's voices from the yard, including my Dad's, I fell asleep and only woke a bit when grandma got into bed. I could hear her slapping cream onto her skin. She only snored a little bit so I soon went back to sleep.

Grandma got up early. There wasn't even any sunshine, just a kind of half light. There was a strange singing coming from nearby, like one voice going up and down and she told me it was the mosque, that people were saying their prayers. My cousin Jocelyn was already up and going to get water from the pump. She said it wasn't far to go so I went with her. We had to wait in the queue for ages with other kids, some of them had walked a very long way, she told me. We filled the yellow plastic container and I helped her put it on her head. It was way too heavy. She tried to put it on me but we were laughing too much. The other kids were looking at me, I suppose because I'm mixed race, light skinned and asking about who was the yellow pikin, but I'm proud of being a bit Polish and a bit African.

Grandma heated up water for me and brought the bucket into the bathroom and gave me a plastic cup. A nice warm bath would have been fantastic but I wasn't going to complain. Dad wanted to make this a happy trip, for me to see all my cousins and family, so I didn't want to go on about stuff. But I know Mummy wouldn't have liked it and would have been on his case, big time.

I played skipping games in the street with Jocelyn and the others, though I couldn't get my tongue around some of the rhymes. It wasn't a real road, like back home, just sort of hard, red earth and lumpy. I watched the cars and people going backwards and forwards and even a big parade, with musicians playing trumpets, horns and rows of drums.

One day passed another and I took pictures on my phone to show my friends (and Mummy if she came to visit me). Uncle Lamin took us to Lumley Beach and we had ice-cream and swam in the sea, though Dad stopped me from going out too far, even though I've got my twenty lengths certificate. One day Dad took us all out to a beautiful beach, that he said was River Number Two. We had a lovely picnic and played in a stream that flowed into the ocean. There was a devil in a big mask and everyone was dancing around him, including Dad and a woman he said was Evelyna, who had travelled in the second car.

Grandma took me and my cousins to church with her on Sunday. My Auntie Lucee came too. She asked me if I had a dress with me to wear as I was always in jeans or shorts or leggings. I had to iron the dress I'd brought with me and clean my shoes. Grandma said she would get take me to the market and get a nice piece of gara cloth, to get a dress made for me. I don't really wear dresses much but I said thank you. I wondered where Dad was and I asked Auntie Lucee if he was coming but she just shook her head and smiled. Church was so loud. The music and singing was nice but it went on for such a long time and the pastor was shouting till my head hurt. Mummy used to take me to church sometimes but it was always very quiet and calm, with candles and we did a lot of kneeling. I made my first holy communion three years ago and had a beautiful white dress with a train. I wondered if Mummy had got some of the photos from that day.

There was a lot of stuff about the devil and I thought of the masked devil on the beautiful beach we went to. I could almost taste the slices of fresh pineapple we ate that day. I smiled thinking of the hills behind the beach that were so full of trees. One of my cousins went to get me a jelly coconut. He slashed off the top and told me to drink the coconut water and scooped out the white coconut jelly from inside. It was almost as cold as ice-cream. Then that made me think about the Evelyna Dad was dancing with. I could see she was very pretty, with a wide smile and her hair falling in soft curls round her face, so that you could hardly see her eyes. She didn't have it braided. So then I said a prayer that she wasn't going to be a new Mummy. If Mummy can't come back, then I wanted it to be just me and Dad.

So I got a shock the next day when Grandma said that Evelyna was going to take me to the market to choose a piece of cloth and I'd get measured up for a nice dress.

'Can't you take me Grandma?'

'Well, I got too much to do. All these people to feed. And the girl who does the washing is coming today.'

Dad turned up later with Evelyna and he pulled this thick wad of notes out of his pocket and gave it to her, to take me to the market. I wondered why he didn't give it to me. I'm sensible with money and I never lose any.

'And get some for yourself too,' he said pressing another wad into her hand. 'I'll catch you later.'

I decided I wasn't going to talk to her all the way to the market, so I concentrated on walking carefully around the drains and traffic. I pretended I couldn't understand what she was saying but really I could. She just smiled and edged me between the stalls till we got to one where bolts of cloth were piled on top of each other.

'Which colour do you like Tasha? This smoky pink one or this blue and green?' I didn't really want to buy any of them but to annoy her I chose a brown one, sort of coffee and cream pattern.

'This is too old for you – choose a nice, bright colour. This pink and blue one would suit you with your pretty skin colour.' She held it out to me with her long red nailed hand but I shook my head, so the stall holder measured out two lapas. Evelyna picked a mauve lacy cloth and held it against herself in front of the mirror. We carried the material to another shop, where the tailor took my measurements. He already had hers but he made some joke about it and she sort of blushed and started laughing.

We'd been there over a week, when Grandma got up from kneeling to say her prayers, sat on the edge of the bed and said. 'I know you miss your Mummy, Tasha. I am praying for you.'

I could feel tears pushing their way up and through my head but I wanted to be brave and anyway, I had done all my crying in secret, away from Dad, but I couldn't help a few tears falling down the side of my cheek. Grandma patted my head. 'You will see her again, I'm sure. But not just now. She has gone home. I don't think she was happy with my son, your father.' She shook her head. 'Perhaps it was a mistake.' She rolled in beside me and put her squashy arm around me. She smelt of smoked fish because she'd been taking the bones out of the ones we brought back from the seaside.

'Maybe,' she said 'Your Daddy will find a new wife here. From his own people.'

I stiffened. What was going on? Were we going to stay here forever and not go back home? But it was so hot all the time and I wanted to see my friends and eat pizza on Friday nights and have sleepovers watching films.

Dad was out a lot because he said he had friends to catch up with. I didn't mind. It was fun spending time with Jocelyn and the others, though they had an awful lot of chores to do but, sometimes, even they were fun, like the day we spent getting the rose apples from the tree in the back yard. But one day he asked me if I'd like to go to Lumley Beach again for an ice cream at Kingdom Hall. So we got a taxi through town, which I nearly knew the way through now, down Campbell St and out beyond the prison and over a bridge and into the wide streets with big houses.

There were lots of colourful stalls on the beach and he asked me if I wanted to buy a present for my best friend, Alicia, so I chose a t shirt with a map of Africa on it and some cowrie shells around the neck. We ate our ice-creams and walked along the sand, watching the lines of fishermen pulling in their huge nets. He stopped to buy some fish for grandma and said

'How are you liking it here Tasha?'

'It's great Dad. I'm having a nice time. But when are we going home?'

'Next week. We fly on Wednesday. Look, there's something I need to tell you.'

My breath stopped.

'Your mummy isn't going to come back. She wants to stay in Poland. I'm sorry but we are not happy together.'

I didn't say anything but I remembered all the rows and shouting and broken plates. I'd told Alicia that home was like a war going on.

'A man needs a wife. A daughter needs a mother.'

'Oh. But we're fine Dad.' I could feel mounting panic. 'I've got a Mummy, even if she doesn't live with me any more.'

'I really like Evelyna. I knew her when I was at secondary school and now we've caught up again. I would like to marry her and bring her to England.'

Well at least we weren't staying here for ever but his news tasted bad in my mouth so I spat on the ground to stop being sick.

'She's a nice lady, isn't she?'

I looked up at his big man's face, his head shining in the sunlight, his eyes looking far out to sea. 'Suppose,' I said and he just patted my head.

'I think you'll get along.'

The whole family got dressed to go to a party to remember an uncle who had died a year ago. Grandma had been cooking for ages and was bringing pepper chicken with her so that the taxi smelt like her kitchen. Of course Evelyna was there, sat right next to Dad. They kept whispering and giggling together. Her skirt was so tight, she could hardly sit down and get up again and her red nails now matched her red lipstick. She kept shaking her head to flick back the long hair off her face and I wondered could it be a wig? It stayed on very well.

I wondered if I willed it hard enough, would she fall down the stone stairs in her high heels and then have to go home, but it didn't work. She came over to me and squatted, I don't know how, and held my chin up to look at me.

'I'll be coming to visit you in London soon Tasha. I hope you are going to show me around all the shops.'

I tried to smile but my mouth became very tight. This was going to call for more than wishes and spells. Later that night, while Grandma was saying her prayers I texted Alicia and told her the problem. Advice needed I said. But all she wrote was, just be horrible to her and she'll go away. She didn't know my Dad that well.

I didn't make up my mind to do it. It just sort of happened. Grandma sent me down to the kiosk on the corner to buy some matches and I looked at the thousand Leone note in my hand. It seemed like a lot of money. I knew it wasn't really because I'd seen my Dad buying an ice-cream with five thousand. Then I saw a Devil dancing down Circular Rd with a crowd of people in costumes singing, dancing, shaking instruments and banging drums and I sort of followed along with a bunch of other kids, trailing at the back. The Devil danced in and out of streets and past the big pink church and down the hill and into an alley way. They wouldn't let the kids follow down so I wandered off in the direction of the church I went to with grandma, least I thought it was, but the houses were so higgledy piggeldy, I got confused. And then I ended up on the busy road that takes you to the normal shops. I recognised some of the big buildings and a stall that sold colourful dresses. It would be nice if I had enough money to buy mummy one. She loves the colour red and these dresses were so bright, blowing around in the breeze like empty rag dolls.

Then the pavements got busier and busier and I had to weave in and out of men in suits, looking like they were coming from important jobs, ladies in beautiful dresses, grown-ups and kids selling things from the bowls and baskets on their heads, carts of men selling green coconuts, kiosks with radios and batteries, playing music, boys changing money, beggars, small boys running around. It was so confusing and hot as.

The smell wasn't nice either. I was so thirsty I bought a small plastic of water from a girl with a tray, selling them at the car windows. There was a tall woman with hair the same colour as mummy's up ahead so I tried to catch up with her, just thinking, just maybe it might be mummy, come to look for me. I ran up beside her and looked up as she looked down and smiled, but she was nothing like her really, and older I think, with a paper file under her arm and a big badge on her shirt.

So then I sat down near the big, big tree, that Dad called the Cotton Tree and he'd taken me to see it one day, talking about history and stuff. I watched all the cars and people pressed up against each other and thought about the day I went shopping in Oxford St with Mummy and she put a shopping bag down and a thief ran off with it so fast, we couldn't catch her. Mummy started shouting in Polish, like she does when she's angry and people stopped and stared. Some people passing by stared at me but I didn't take any notice of them. And then a man with no arms came by begging for money and I felt frightened. I know it's not right to be scared of people who are disabled but I did, so I sort of folded myself into the bench. Then another boy, older than me, sat down beside me. He was wearing a torn t shirt and broken flip flops and started talking to me, but I could only get bits and pieces. He worked out I wasn't local so he said

'You must get money. Gi mi one thousand.'

But I just shook my head and he started to get angry and

grabbed at the pockets in my jeans, so I pushed and slid out of his grasp and ran along the street, feeling him behind me, but I was in trainers and he was in flip flops, also I was smaller and could get through the crowds more easily. Then I ran out of breath and leaned against the wall of an old church. It was beginning to get dark now and I didn't know where I was. At the bottom of the sloping street opposite, I thought I could see water, so that must be the ocean. It was going to be cooler, close to the sea, so I crossed over and walked down past a café. There were a lot of white people coming in and out, and big cars in the street with their lights on. I wondered if Dad knew I was missing now and lost. Would he be looking for me or busy spending time with Evelyna? I knew he was going to be mad as when he found me. Was Grandma Claudia worrying about me? It looked so dark at the bottom of the street, I was afraid to go on and there were so many beggars around the café, bothering the people coming in and out. They looked so poor. Some were on crutches. One man had only one leg. Some of the rich people coming out the café gave them money and others just walked past to their big cars. I went up to one woman and touched her on the arm. Perhaps she would help me get back to Grandma's but she must have thought I was begging too and brushed my hand away. I felt a tear in my eye and the crowd of beggars were muttering bad words at me. Back up the hill, on the main road, the tears were coming out faster now but in the crowd no-one could see and I couldn't see very well so I bumped into a girl the same height as me, with a red plastic container on her head.

'Na wetin matter wit yu? She said.

'Sorry,' I said.

She looked at my face and the tears were falling now. Hers was round and very dark and shiny and she he had big round eyes and dimples in her cheeks. She touched my arm. 'Kam,' she said and we went up a side street where a woman was sat behind a stall. They talked in a language that wasn't even Krio.

The girl took the red plastic container off her head and wound down the piece of cloth it had been balanced on.

'No cry ya,' she said 'Kam sidohn.'

'I'm lost. I don't know how to get home.'

'We yu fambul dehn?' I knew she was asking about my family so I told them about my Grandma, Mrs. Claudia Kamara and I remembered the name of the street. They talked to each other in their language and the girl pulled out a piece of what she was selling. 'Kaya', she said and snapped me off a bit. It was really sweet. 'A nem Rugiatu,' she said. I told her my name was Natasha. 'Yu kin sho mi di rod,' she said, pulling me up by the arm. She lifted the red container on her head and we started walking up along the busy main street. We walked in the dark, stepping over storm drains and round stalls, between people walking and people selling, until we came to the street with the bright pink church. I told her we were not too far. She was stopping every once in a while to shout 'I geh de kaya fe sale' and a few people stopped to buy from her. As we climbed the hill, we got closer to Grandma's and I pointed to the house, when we got to the end of the street. She turned to look at me, smiled and pointed at my trainers.

'Gi mi di krep, nor ya?'

She had a pair of flip flops on and I had another pair of shoes in the suitcase. I thought, well, Dad's going to be so happy to see me he's not going to be annoyed I gave my Nikes away, so I slipped them off and ran towards Grandma Claudia's yellow house. I could hear Rugiatu shouting thankyou as she walked back the way she came, with the red container of peanut biscuits on her head, and holding the rubber flip flops in her left hand.

Acknowledgments

'Odelia' was published in *Platform, New Fiction by North East Writers*, ed. Olivia Chapman, pub. New Writing North

'Snow on Snow' was published in *The Possibility of Bears* ed. Brian Lister, Biscuit Publishing

'Goebbels' House' won 2nd prize in Ilkley Literature Festival Competition and was published in *Root,* ed. Kitty Fitzgerald, Iron Press

'The Visiting Room' was published in The Journal and also an excerpt in Orbis Magazine.

'Oasis' was published in Isis Arts anthology *Home*

'The Frock', under the title of 'The Ice Fairy' was published by Comma Press in *Newcastle Stories* ed. Angela Readman

'What You Need for Happiness' was published in *The Devil's Bathtub* ed. Brian Lister, Biscuit Publishing

With thanks to Dot Lee, Ezekiel Williams and John Murray for their support and advice.

Thanks to my publisher Sheila Wakefield.

Biography

Pauline Plummer was born in Liverpool but has lived in the North East of England since 1982. She has taught in Poland, Sierra Leone and Greece. She has worked as a tutor of creative writing for the last twenty years and is also a founding editor of Mudfog Press. She has published five collections of poetry, including the most recent *From Here to Timbukto* (Smokestack Press) which was a novella in verse. In recent years she has become increasingly interested in telling stories and her prize-winning stories have been published in anthololgies (Comma Press, Iron Press, New Writing North, Isis Arts, Biscuit Publishing and Mudfog presses, The Journal newspaper). Her previous short story *Manifesto* was read at Northern Stage as part of the fifty year celebration of *Look Back in Anger*.

Stories with strong cross-cultural themes written in engaging prose about people and how they love and live wherever they find themselves. They explore friendships and misunderstandings, loss and reconciliation; a mother visits her bi-racial son in prison, a lonely woman begins an affair with a Zimbabwean student she meets on a train, an ageing Hungarian refugee needs to sell his house, a girl on VSO in West Africa finds herself confronted by her own inadequacies, the young daughter of an Irish immigrant family in the 50s longs for a pretty dress, a woman drifts into prostitution in the hotels of West London. The stories are often tender sometimes rueful and bitter-sweet.

Pauline Plummer